Pilgrim's Progress

One Syllable Adventure Series

Pilgrim's Progress

SYLLABLE 1

John Bunyan

Bridge-Logos *Publishers*

Gainesville, Florida 32614 USA

One Syllable Adventure Series: The Pilgrim's Progress

Copyright © 2003
by Bridge-Logos

International Standard Book Number: 0-88270-9380
Library of Congress Catalog Card Number:

Published by:

Bridge-Logos
Gainesville, FL 32614
bridgelogos.com

GENE FEDELE has been writing, editing, and publishing for 21 years. He has designed numerous Christian books and magazines, including the Pilgrim's Progress: In Words of One Syllable, the Great Christian Biographies series, and Robert Murray M'Cheyne: Unpublished Poetry and Prose. Gene has been the founding editor and publisher of the Christian Family Journal since 1998. The magazine is distributed to Christians in 16 countries.

Jo: Bunyan 1682

CONTENTS

PART I.

PART II.

PREFACE

"Suffer the little children to come unto me, for of such is the kingdom of Heaven."? Mark 10:14

To the Children;

The life of a child is but a seed, from which great things for God in time may sprout. The face of each child who trusts in Christ says: "I will bless the lives of all whom I touch, for they will find rest and hope in me. The weak will sit in the shade of my strength. I will bring joy to the hearts filled with pain and grief. I will speak words of God's love and grace in the ears of lost ones. And I will shine forth the full light of the King."

Some may say, "But how? You are a frail child. How can you do such grand things?" And then you will say, "Yes, I may be small, but I can do all things through Christ, who gives me strength." "But," some child may say, "I have no gifts to give for Christ." "And there are some who think they are too small or simple or weak to live for such a great God." Yet there is no doubt that Christ's great love for each child will shine though the days be dark or the pain be sore, and those in plain view can see but little.

It is like the true tale of a man who once came to Amsterdam to hear the famed tunes of the chimes of St. Nicholas. He went up to the church to hear sweet tunes in his ears, and there he found an old man who wore gloves made of wood on his hands. The old man struck the keys with all his might, but all that was heard was the clash of the gloves on the keys and the harsh noise of the bells close to the man's head. The man thought, "Why has there been so much talk about the chimes of St. Nicholas? Have I come here in vain?" For to him there were no sweet sounds in them.

Yet, all the while, there soared to all far off in the towns and plains, a sound so sweet and full of joy. Men at work in the fields paused to listen and were made glad. Folks in their homes were thrilled by the notes that fell from the chimes.

So there are some lives which to those who dwell close to them, seem to make no sweet sounds. But whose lives are in truth, full of love and joy if just given the chance to shine.

It is my hope and prayer that this sweet tale of Christian and Christiana might lead you on the path that they tread in this life. They fought off not a few foes on their trek to the Celestial City.

In the words of this book you will see how Christian beat the foul fiend Apollyon by faith in Christ in his heart and the sword of the Word of God in his hand. The scene of Christian and Hopeful in the dark cell of Doubting Castle shows the love of God for all who use the key of God's pledge that He will not leave us. Pilgrim's Progress is a tale that shows the truths of the path of this life which leads to the life to come.

My sweet son, Christopher, loved to read Pilgrim's Progress even the last days of his life. He loved to do what Jesus would want him to, as well. His trust was in God when he felt pain in his arms, legs or head. When he had to have blood drawn from his arm, he would first ask us all to pray to God with him for strength. Though his life on earth was just eight short years, he showed the love and grace of God in his heart like one who was old and gray. In short, his own life and faith is a proof that through each child God works great things in this world and moves the hearts of boys and girls, like you, to live their life in Christ. He wants your heart and He wants you to trust Him to do what is best.

May the love of Jesus reign in your soul,

From Christopher's Dad

DEDICATION

I humbly dedicate this edition of *Pilgrim's Progress* to my only son, CHRISTOPHER JOHN FEDELE (1990-1998), who, in the span of his life upon this earth, exemplified the character of Christian more than anyone I have ever known. His faith in his Savior was, undoubtedly, the sustaining power amidst every moment of his suffering during the course of his four year battle against leukemia. He has touched and continues to influence—for deeper holiness and constant reflection on the glories of eternity—the lives of everyone who knew him. He now stands victorious with his Savior and all the Saints who went before him, awaiting the rest of us to join him forever in everlasting peace and joy. O, what a thought! O, what a sight! I can hardly wait...

"Eye hath not seen, nor ear heard, nor have entered into the heart of man the things which God hath prepared for those that love Him."
—1 Corinthians 2:9

Gene Fedele
Managing Editor

The PILGRIMS PROGRESS

PART I

Stage One

As I went through the wild waste of this world, I came to a place where there was a den, and I laid down in it to sleep. While I slept, I had a dream, and lo! I saw a man whose clothes were in rags, and he stood with his face turned from his own house, with a book in his hand, and a great load on his back. I saw him read from the leaves of the book, and as he read, he wept and shook with fear; and soon he broke out with a loud cry and said, "What shall I do to save my soul?"

So in his plight he went home, and as long as he could he held his peace, that his wife and babes should not see his grief. But at length he told them his mind and said, "O, my dear wife, and you my babes, I your dear friend, am full of woe, for a load lies hard on me; and more than this, I have been told that our town will be burnt with fire; in which I, you my wife, and you my sweet babes, shall be lost, if means are not found to save us."

The man mourns over his sin and fear.

This sad tale struck all who heard him with awe, not that they thought what he said to them was true, but that they had fears that some great weight must be on his mind. So as night now drew near, they hoped that sleep and rest might soothe his brain, and with all haste they got him in to bed.

When the morn broke, they sought to know how he did. He told them, "worse and worse"; and he set to speak to them again in the same way as he had done; but they did not want to hear of it. So to drive off his words, they spoke harsh things to him; at times they would laugh, and at times they would chide, and then they sent him out. So he went to his room to pray for them, as well as to nurse his own grief. He would go, too,

in the woods to read and think, and for some weeks he spent his time in this way.

Now I saw in my dreams, that one day as he took his walk in the fields with his book in his hands, he gave a deep groan—for he felt as if a cloud were on his soul—and he burst out as he was apt to do and said, "Who will save me?" I saw that he gave wild looks this way and that, as if he would rush off; yet he stood still, for he could not tell which way was the best to go. At last, a man, whose name was Evangelist, came up to him and said, "Why do you weep?"

He said, "Sir, I see by this book in my hand that I am to die, and that then God will judge me, and I dread this death."

EVANGELIST: Why do you fear death, since this life is filled with grief and pain?

He seeks to flee the wrath to come.

THE MAN: I fear a hard doom should wait me, and that this load on my back should make me sink down, till at last, I shall find I am in hell.

EVANGELIST: If this be your case, then why do you stand here still?

THE MAN: I know not where to go.

Then Evangelist gave him a scroll with these words on it: "Flee from the wrath to come."

The man read it and said, "Which way must I go?" Evangelist held out his hand to point to a gate in a wide field and said, "Do you see The Wicket Gate?"

THE MAN: No.

EVANGELIST: Do you see that light?

THE MAN: I think I do.

EVANGELIST: Keep that light in your eye, and go straight up to it. When you come up to the gate, you shall knock, and then it shall be told you what you are to do.

Then I saw in my dream that Christian—for that was his name—set off to run. Now he had not gone far from his own door, when his wife and young ones, who saw him, gave a loud wail to beg him to come back; but the man put his hands in his ears, and ran on with a cry of "Life! Life!" The friends of his wife came out to see him run, and as he went some mocked him, some used threats, and there were two, named Obstinate and Pliable, who set off to fetch him back by force. Now, by this time, the man had gone a good way off, but since his load was so great, they at last caught up with him.

Then said Christian, "Friends, why have you come?"

"To bid you to go back with us," they said.

"But that can by no means be! You dwell in The City of Destruction, the place where I, too, was born. I know it to be so, and there you will die and sink down to a place which burns with fire. Be wise, good friends, and come with me."

Pliable and Obstinate give chase to Christian.

"What? Leave our goods, and all our wealth and friends?"

"Yes," said Christian, "for all which you might leave is but a grain to that which I seek, and if you will go with me and hold it firm, you shall fare as well as I; for there, where I go, you will find all you want and more to spare. Come with me, and see if it be true."

OBSTINATE: What are the things you seek, since you leave all the world to find them?

CHRISTIAN: I seek those joys that fade not, which are laid up in a place of bliss—safe there for those who go in search of them. Read it here, if you will, in my book.

OBSTINATE: Off with your book! Will you go back with us or not?

CHRISTIAN: No, not I, for I have made up my mind to go on.

OBSTINATE: Come, friend Pliable, let us turn back and leave him; there is a troop of such fools who, when they go with a whim, are more wise in their own eyes than ten men who know how to think.

PLIABLE: No, do not scorn him if what the good Christian says is true, the things he looks to are of more worth than ours: my heart leans to what he says.

OBSTINATE: What? More fools still! Go back, back, and be wise.

CHRISTIAN: No, but do come with your friend Pliable for there are such things to be had as those I just spoke of, and more too. See here! Read in this book which comes to us from God, who could not lie.

PLIABLE: Well, friend Obstinate, I think I know what to do; and I mean to go with this good man, and to cast my lot in with his.

Then said he to Christian, "Do you know the way to the place you speak of?"

CHRISTIAN: I am told by a man whose name is Evangelist to do my best to reach a gate that is in front of us, where I shall be told how to find the way.

Obstinate goes back. Pliable goes on with Christian.

So they went on side by side.

OBSTINATE: And I will go back to my own home. I will not go with such vain folk as you.

Now I saw in my dream that when Obstinate had gone back, Christian and Pliable set off to cross the plain, and they spoke as they went:

CHRISTIAN: Well, Pliable, how do you do now? I am glad you have a mind to go with me.

PLIABLE: Come, friend Christian, tell me more of the things of which we go in search.

CHRISTIAN: I can find them in my heart, though I find it hard to speak of them with my tongue; but yet, since you wish to know, this book tells us of a world that has no bounds, and a life that has no end.

PLIABLE: Well said, and what else?

CHRISTIAN: That there are crowns of light in store for us and robes that will make us shine like the sun.

PLIABLE: This is good; and what else?

PLIABLE

CHRISTIAN: That there shall be no more cares nor grief, for the Lord that owns the place will wipe all tears from our eyes.

PLIABLE: And what friends shall we find there?

CHRISTIAN: There we shall be with all the saints, in robes so bright that our eyes will grow dim to look on them. There shall we meet those who in this world have stood out for the faith, and have been burnt on the stake, and thrown to wild beasts, for the love they bore to the Lord. They will not harm us, but will greet us with love, for they all walk in the sight of God.

PLIABLE: But how shall we get to share all this?

CHRISTIAN: The Lord of that land said, if we wish to gain that world it shall be ours if we ask.

PLIABLE: Well, my good friend, I am glad to hear of these things. Come on, let us move our pace.

CHRISTIAN: I can not go as fast as I would like, for this load on my back weighs me down.

Then I saw in my dream that just as they had come to an end of this talk, they drew near to a slough that was in the midst of the plain, and as they took no heed, they both fell in. The name of the slough was Despond. Here they laid for a time in the mud; and the load that Christian had on his back made him sink all the more in the mire.

Man's sin makes the Slough of Despond.

PLIABLE: Ah! friend Christian, where are we now?

CHRISTIAN: In truth, I do not know.

Then Pliable said to his friend, "Is this the bliss of which you have told me all this time? If we have such ill speed when we first set out, what may we look for on the rest of our way?" And with that he got out of the mire on that side of the slough which was next to his own house; then off he went, and Christian saw him no more.

So Christian was left to strive in the Slough of Despond as well as he could; yet his aim was to reach that side of the slough that was next to The Wicket Gate, which at last he did, but he could not get out for

the load that was on his back. Then I saw in my dream
that a man came to him whose name was Help.

"Why are you in here?" said Help.

CHRISTIAN: I was bid to go this way by Evangelist,
who told me to pass up to the gate, that I
might flee from the wrath to come, and on my
way to it I fell in this slough.

Help gives
aid to
Christian.

HELP: But why did you not look for the steps?

CHRISTIAN: Fear came so hard on me that I fled the
next way and fell in.

HELP: Give me your hand.

So he gave him his hand, and he drew him out, and
set him on firm ground, and sent him on his way.

Then in my dream I went up to Help and said to

him, "Sir, since this place is on the way from The City of Destruction to The Wicket Gate, how is it that no one mends this patch of ground, so that those who come by may not fall in the slough?"

HELP: This slough is such a place as no one can mend. It is the spot which runs the scum and filth that wait on sin, and that is why men call it the Slough of Despond. When the man of sin wakes up to a sense of his own lost state, doubts and fears rise up in his soul, and all of them drain down and sink in this place: and it is this that makes the ground so bad. True there are good and sound steps in the midst of the slough, but at times it is hard to see them; or if they be seen, men's heads are so dull that they step on one side and fall in the mire. But the ground is good once they have come in at the gate.

Now I saw in my dream that by this time Pliable had gone back to his house once more, and that his friends came to see him: some said how wise it was to come home, and some that he was a fool to have gone. Some, too, mocked him, who said, "Well, if I had set out as you, I would not have been such a fool as to come back due to a slough in the road. So Pliable was left to sneak off; but at last he gained more heart, and then all were heard to turn their taunts and laugh at poor Christian.

Worldly Wiseman meets Christian.

Now as Christian went on his way he saw a man come through the field to meet him, whose name was Mr. Worldly Wiseman, and he dwelt in the town of Carnal Policy, which was near that town from where Christian came. He had heard some news of Christian, for his flight from The City of Destruction had made much noise, and was now the talk far and near. So he said, "Good Sir, where do you go with such a load on your back?"

MR. WORLDLY WISEMAN

CHRISTIAN: It is a load, for sure; and if you ask me where I go, I must tell you, Sir, I must go to The Wicket Gate in front of me, for there I shall be put in a way to rid me of my load.

WORLDLY WISEMAN: Have you not a wife and babes?

CHRISTIAN: Yes, but with this load I do not seem to care for them as I did; and in truth, I feel as if I had none.

WORLDLY WISEMAN: Will you hear me if I speak my mind to you?

CHRISTIAN: If what you say be good, I will, for I stand much in need of help.

WORLDLY WISEMAN: I would urge you then, with all speed, to get rid of your load; for your mind will not be at rest till then.

CHRISTIAN: That is just what I seek to do. But there

is no man in our land who can take it off me.

WORLDLY WISEMAN: Who sent you to go this way to be rid of it?

CHRISTIAN: One that I took to be a great and true man; his name is Evangelist.

WORLDLY WISEMAN: Hark at what I say! There is no worse way in the world than that which he has sent you, which you will find if you take him for your guide. In this short time you have met with bad luck, for I see the mud of the Slough of Despond is on your coat. Hear me, for I have seen more of the world than you. In the way you go you will meet with pain, woe, thirst, and even the sword—in a word, death! Take no heed of what Evangelist tells you.

Worldly Wiseman shuns Evangelist's words.

CHRISTIAN: Why, Sir, this load on my back is worse to me than all those things which you speak of; no, I care not what I meet with in the way, if I can get rid of my load.

WORLDLY WISEMAN: How did you come by it at first?

CHRISTIAN: Why, I read this book.

WORLDLY WISEMAN: Like more weak men I know, who aim at things too high for them, you have lost heart, and run in the dark at great risk, to gain who knows what!

CHRISTIAN: I know what I would gain, it is ease for my load.

WORLDLY WISEMAN: But why will you seek ease in this way, when I could put you on the path to gain it where there would be no risk; and the cure is at hand?

CHRISTIAN: Pray, Sir, tell me what that way is.

WORLDLY WISEMAN: Well, in the next town, which you can see from here—the name of which is Morality—there lives a man whose name is Legality, a wise man, and a man of some rank, who has skill to help men off with such loads as yours from their backs. I know he has done a great deal of good in that way; and he has the skill to cure those who, from the loads they bear, are not quite sound in their wits. To him you may go and get help. His house is but a mile from this place, and should he not be at home, he has a son whose name is Civility, who can do it just as well. There, I say, you may go to get rid of your load. I would not have you go back to your old home, but you can send for your wife and babes, and you will find that food there is cheap and good.

Christian snared by Worldly Wiseman's false words.

Now Christian was brought to a stand, and he said, "Sir, which is the way to this good man's house?"

WORLDLY WISEMAN: Do you see that hill?

CHRISTIAN: Yes, I do.

WORLDLY WISEMAN: By that hill you must go, and the first house you come to is his.

So Christian went out of his way to find Mr. Legality's house to seek help. But when he had gone close up the hill, it was so steep and high that he had fears lest it should fall on his head; so he stood still, as he knew not what to do. His load, too, was of more weight to him than when he was on the right road. Then came flames of fire out of the hill, that made him quake for fear lest he should be burnt. And now it was a great grief to him that he had lent his ear to Worldly Wiseman; and it was well that he just then saw Evangelist come to meet him; though at the sight of him he felt a deep blush creep on his face for shame. So Evangelist drew near, and when he came up to him, he said, with a sad look, "Why are you here, Christian?"

Evangelist shows Christian his error.

To these words Christian knew not what to say, so he stood still. Then Evangelist went on thus: "Are you not the man that I heard cry in The City of Destruction?"

CHRISTIAN: Yes, dear Sir, I am the man.

EVANGELIST: Did I not point out to you the way to The Wicket Gate?

CHRISTIAN: Yes, you did, Sir.

EVANGELIST: How is it, then, that you have so soon gone out of the way?

CHRISTIAN: When I came out of the Slough of Despond, I met a man who told me that in a town near I might find one who could take off my load.

EVANGELIST: Who was he?

CHRISTIAN: He had fair looks and said much to me, and got me at last to yield, so I came here. But when I saw this hill, and how steep it was, I made a stand, lest it should fall on my head.

EVANGELIST: What did the man say to you?

When Evangelist had heard from Christian all that took place, he said, "Stand still a while, that I may show you the words of God."

So Evangelist went on to read, "Now the just shall live by faith, but if a man draw back, my soul shall have no joy in him." "Is not this the case with you?" he said. "Have you not drawn back your feet from the way of peace, to your own cost; and do you not spurn the most high God?"

Then Christian fell down at his feet as dead, and said, "Woe is me! Woe is me!"

At the sight of this, Evangelist caught him by the right hand and said, "Faith hopes all things."

Then Christian found some peace and stood up.

EVANGELIST: I pray that you give more heed to the things that I shall tell you. The Lord says, "Strive to go in at the Strait Gate, the gate to which I send you, for strait is the gate that leads to life, and few there be that find it." Why did you not hear the words of God, for the sake of Mr. Worldly Wiseman? That is, in truth, the right name for him. The Lord has told you that he "who will save his life shall lose it." He to whom you were sent for ease, Legality by name, could not set you free—no man yet has got rid of his load through him; he could but show you the way to woe, for by the deeds of the law no man can be rid of his load. So that Mr. Worldly Wiseman and his friend Mr. Legality are false guides; and as for his son Civility, he could not help you.

Mr. Legality and Civility are false guides.

Now Christian, in great dread, could think of one thing—death—and sent forth a sad cry in grief that he had gone from the right way. Then he spoke once more to Evangelist in these words: "Sir, what do you think? Is there hope for me? May I now go back, and strive to reach The Wicket Gate? I grieve that I gave ear to this man's voice, but may my sin find grace?

EVANGELIST: Your sin is great, for you have gone from the way that is good, to tread in false paths, yet the man at the gate will let you through, for he has love and good will for all men; but take heed that you turn not to the right hand or to the left.

Stage Two

hen Christian made a move to go back, but Evangelist gave him a kiss and a smile, and bade him God speed.

So he went on with haste and did not speak on the road, and could not feel safe till he was in the path which he had left. In time, he came up to the gate. He saw by the words which he read on it, that those who would knock could go in, so he gave two or three knocks, and said, "May I now go in here?

Will you open to me, though I have been a poor wretch? Then I shall not fail to sing His praises on high."

At last there came a grave man to the gate, whose name was Good-will, and he said, "Who is there? Where do you come from, and what do you want?"

CHRISTIAN: I come from The City of Destruction with a load of sins on my back. I am on my way to Mount Zion, that I may be free from the wrath to come. And as I have been told that my way is through this gate, I ask, Sir, will you let me in?

GOOD-WILL: With all my heart.

So he flung back the gate and pulled Christian in.

Satan hates those who enter at the Strait Gate.

Then said Christian: "What does that mean?" Good-will told him that a short way from this gate there was a strong fort of which Beelzebub was the chief. He and the rest that dwelt there shot darts at those that came up to the gate to try to kill them if they could.

Then said Christian: "I come in with joy and with fear." So when he had gone in, the man at the gate said, "Who sent you here?"

CHRISTIAN: Evangelist urged me come and knock, as I did, and he said that you, Sir, would tell me what I must do.

GOOD-WILL: The door is thrown back wide for you to come in, and no man can shut it.

CHRISTIAN: Now I seem to reap the good of all the risks I have met with on the way.

GOOD-WILL: But how is it that no one comes with you?

CHRISTIAN: None of my friends saw that there was cause of fear, as I did.

GOOD-WILL: Did they know of your flight?

CHRISTIAN: Yes, my wife and young ones saw me go, and I heard their cries as they ran out to try and stop me. Some of my friends, too, would have had me come home, but I put my hands to my ears and went on my way.

GOOD-WILL: But did none of them come out to beg of you to go back?

CHRISTIAN: Yes, both Obstinate and Pliable came, but when they found that I would not yield, Obstinate went home, but Pliable came with me as far as the Slough of Despond.

GOOD-WILL: Why did he not come through it?

When Christian told him the rest, he said: "Ah, poor man! Is a world of bliss such a small thing to him, that he did not think it worth while to run a few risks to gain it?"

Then he told Good-will how he had been led from the straight path by Mr. Worldly Wiseman.

GOOD-WILL: Oh, he did lead you on? He would have had you seek ease at the hands of Mr. Legality. In truth, they are both cheats. And did you take heed of what he said?

Christian then told him all. "But now that I am come," said he, "I am more fit for death than to stand

and talk to my Lord. But oh, the joy it is to me to be here!"

GOOD-WILL: We keep none out that knock at this gate. They may have sinned at times on the way, yet they are "in no wise cast out." So, good Christian, come with me, and I will teach you the way you must go. Look in front. That is the way which was laid down by Christ and the wise men of old, and it is as straight as a rule can make it.

CHRISTIAN: But is there no turn or bend by which one who does not know the road might lose his way?

GOOD-WILL: My friend, there are not a few that lead down to it, and these paths are wide: yet by this you may know the right from the wrong—the right are straight and are by no means wide.

Then I saw in my dream that Christian said, "Could you not help me off with this load on my back?"—as yet he had not been rid of it. He was told: "As to your load, you must bear it till you come to the place of Deliverance, for there it will fall from your back."

The blood of Christ alone can rid the guilt of sin.

Then Christian would have set off on the road, but Good-will said, "Stop a while and let me tell you that when you have gone through the gate you will see the house of Mr. Interpreter, at whose door you must knock, and he will show you good things. Then Christian took leave of his friend, who bade him God speed.

He then went on till he came to the house of Mr.

Interpreter. He knocked two or three times, and at last one came to the door and said: "Who is there?"

CHRISTIAN: I have come to see the good man of the house.

So in a short time Mr. Interpreter came to him and said, "What would you have?"

Christian comes to the house of Interpreter.

CHRISTIAN: Sir, I am come here from The City of Destruction and am on my way to Mount Zion. I was told by the man that stands at the gate, that if I came here you would show me good things that would help me.

Then Interpreter took Christian to a room, and asked his man to bring a light, and there he saw on the wall the print of one who had a grave face, whose eyes were cast up to the sky, and the best of books was in His hand, the law of truth was on His lips, and the world was at His back. He stood as if He would plead for men, and a crown of gold hung near His head.

CHRISTIAN: What does this mean?

INTERPRETER: I have shown you this print first, for this is He who is to be your sole guide when you can not find your way to the land to which you go; so, take heed to what I have shown you, lest you meet with some who would lead you wrong; but their way goes down to death.

Then he took him to a large room that was full of dust, for it had not been swept; and Interpreter told his man to sweep it. Now when he did so, such clouds of dust flew up that it made Christian choke.

Then said Interpreter to a maid that stood by: "Make the floor moist that the dust may not rise; and when she had done this, it was swept with ease."

CHRISTIAN: What does this mean?

INTERPRETER: This room is the heart of that man who knows not the grace of God. The dust is his first sin and the vice that is in him. He that swept first is the Law, but she who made the floor moist is The Book which tells Good News to all men. Now as soon as you saw the first of these sweep, the dust did so fly that the room could not be made clean by him; this is to show you that the law as it works does not cleanse the heart from sin, but gives strength to sin, so as to rouse it up in the soul.

Then you saw the maid come in to calm the dust; so is sin made clean and laid low by faith in The Book.

Now I saw in my dream that Interpreter took Christian by the hand and led him to a small room where two boys sat, each in his chair. Their names were Passion and Patience. Passion seemed quite glum, but Patience was very quiet and full of peace.

CHRISTIAN: Why is Passion so sad?

INTERPRETER: The head of the house would have him wait for his best things till the start of the next year, but he wants to have them all now. While Patience is pleased to wait.

Then I saw that one came to Passion, and brought him a bag, which was filled with toys, and poured it down at his feet. He took it up and laughed Patience to scorn. While I watched, his toys soon went to waste, and he had none left to him but rags. And so it shall be with all such men at the end of this world.

CHRISTIAN: Now I see Patience chose the best way, for he waits for the best things to come. *Passion will have it now, but Patience will wait.*

INTERPRETER: The light of the next world will never wear out, but these are soon gone.

CHRISTIAN: I see it is not right to yearn for things that are now, but wait for things to come.

INTERPRETER: You speak the truth.

"Now," said Christian, "let me go on."

"No," said Interpreter, "not till I have shown you more, then you shall go on your way." So he took Christian by the hand, and led him to a dark room, where there sat a man in a cage.

Now the man looked quite sad. He sat with eyes down and hands clasped. His sighs were such as would break his heart.

The Christian said, "What does this mean?" At which Interpreter asked him to speak with the man.

Then said Christian to the man, "Who are you?"

The man answered, "I am what I was once not."

CHRISTIAN: What were you?

MAN: I was once one who taught, both in my own eyes, and also in the eyes of man. I was once, as I thought, fair for the Celestial City, and had then even joy at the thoughts that I should get there.

CHRISTIAN: Well, but what are you now?

MAN: I am now a man of lost hope, and am shut up in this cage, and I can not get out!

CHRISTIAN: But how did you come to this place?

MAN: I have left off the watch; I have laid the reins on the neck of my lusts. My sin was towards God and His Word; I have grieved the Spirit, and He has left me. I have such a hard heart and I can not repent.

Then said Christian to Interpreter, "But is there no hope for such a man as this?"

"Ask him," said Interpreter.

CHRISTIAN: Can you be set free? Must you be kept in this cage of lost hope?

MAN: I have no hope to be free.

CHRISTIAN: Why not? The Son of the Blessed is full of pity.

MAN: I have hung Him on His cross daily. I have

left Him and caused pain to the Spirit of Grace; and I am now none of His.

CHRISTIAN: But can you not now turn?

MAN: God will not grant me this. He has shut me up in this cage, and all the men in the world can not let me out! Oh, the pain! How shall I meet Him in the last day!

INTERPRETER: Christian, do not forget what you see here.

CHRISTIAN: God help me to watch and pray that I may shun the cause of this man's grief. Sir, is it not time for me to go on my way now?

"Well," said Interpreter, "keep all these things in your mind and heart that they may urge you on, and may faith guide you."

Stage Three

hen I saw in my dream that the high way which Christian was to tread had a wall on each side, and the name of that wall was Salvation. Up this high way did Christian run, but with great pain from the load on his back. He ran till he drew near to a place on which stood a cross at the foot of a tomb. Just as Christian came up to the cross, his load slid from his back, close to the mouth of the tomb,

Christian comes to the cross and is rid of his load.

where it fell in, and I saw it no more.

Then was Christian glad, and said with a heart of joy, "He gives me rest by His grief, and life by His death."

Yet he stood still for a while, for he was struck with awe to think that the sight of the cross should ease him of his load. Three or four times he looked on the cross and the tomb, and tears rose in his eyes.

As he stood and wept, three Bright Ones came to him, and one of them said, "Peace be to you! For you have been saved from your sins." And one came up to him to strip him of his rags and put a new robe on him, while the third set a mark on his face, and gave him a scroll with a seal on it and urged him to look on it as he ran, and give it in when he reached The Celestial City. Then the Bright Ones left him.

Christian gave three leaps for joy, and sang as he went: "I came this far with a load of sin on my back and grief in my heart. Ah, what a place is this! Here did the strings break that bound my load to me. Blessed cross! Blessed tomb! Blessed is the Lord that was put to shame for me!"

A Christian can sing when God gives him joy.

He went on till he came to a vale where he saw three men who were in a sound sleep, with chains on their feet. The name of one was Simple, one Sloth, and the third Presumption. As Christian saw them lie in this place, he went to wake them, and said: "You are like those that sleep on the top of a mast, for the Dead Sea is at your feet. Wake, rise, and come with me! Trust

me, and I will help you off with your chains." He told them, if he that goes to and fro to seek and kill comes by, you will become his prey. With that they cast their eyes up to look at him, and Simple said, "I would like to have more sleep." Presumption said, "Let each man look to his own." And so they laid down to sleep once more, and Christian went on his way.

ien I saw in my dream that two men leapt from
top of the wall and made great haste to come up
to him. Their names were Formalist
and Hypocrisy.

CHRISTIAN: Sirs, from where do
you come, and where do you go?

FORMALIST AND HYPOCRISY: We
were born in the land of Vain-glory,
and are on our way to Mount Zion
for praise.

CHRISTIAN: Why did you
not come in at the gate? Don't
you know that he who does not
come in at the door, but climbs up
to get in, is a thief?

FORMALIST

They told him that to go through the gate was

One must
come
through the
gate.

much too long and that the best way was to
take a short cut, and climb the wall, as they
had done.

CHRISTIAN: But what will the Lord of the town to
which we are bound think of it, if we do not go in the
way of His will?

They told Christian that he need not care on that
score, for a long time it had been made law, and they
could prove that it had been so for years.

CHRISTIAN: But are you quite sure that your ways
will stand up to the law?

"Yes," they said, "no doubt of it. And if we get in the
road at all, pray what are the odds? If we are in, we are

in. Are you not in the way, who comes in at the gate? And we too are in the way that choose to climb the wall. Is not our case as good as yours?"

CHRISTIAN: I walk by the rule of my Lord, but you walk by the rule of your own lusts. The Lord of the way will count you as thieves, and you will not be found true men in the end.

I saw then that they all went on till they came to the foot of the Hill of Difficulty, where there was a spring. There was in the same place two more ways, one on the left hand and one on the right; but the path that Christian was told to take went straight up the hill, and its name was Difficulty, and he saw that was the way of life.

Christian comes to the Hill of Difficulty.

Now when Christian got as far as the Spring of Life he drank of it, and then went up the hill. But when the two men saw that it was steep and high and that there were three ways to choose from, one of them took the path which is named Danger, and lost his way in a great wood. And one of them went by the road of Destruction, which led him to a wide field full of dark rocks, where he fell and rose no more. I then saw Christian go up the hill, where at first I could see him run, then walk, and then go on his hands and knees, for it was so steep. Now half way up was a cave made by the Lord of the hill, that those who came by might rest there.

So Christian sat down and took out the scroll and

Christian drops his scroll.

read it, till at last he fell off in a deep sleep which kept him there till it was dark; and while he slept his scroll fell from his hand. Then a man came up to him and woke him, and said, "Go to the ant, you man of sloth, and learn of her to be wise."

At this Christian sped on his way, at a quick pace. When he came near to the top of the hill, two men ran up to meet him, whose names were Timorous and Mistrust, to whom Christian said, "Sirs, why do you run the wrong way?"

Timorous said that Zion was the hill they meant to climb, but that when they made it half way they found that they met with more and more risk, so

MISTRUST

that great fear came on them, and all they could do was to turn back.

"Yes," said Mistrust, "for just in front of us there lay two beasts of prey in our path; we did not know if they slept or not, but we thought that they would fall on us and tear us limb from limb."

CHRISTIAN: You rouse my fears. Where must I fly to be safe? If I go back to my own town (Destruction) I am sure to lose my life, but if I can get to The Celestial City, there I shall be safe. To turn back is death, to go on is fear of death; but when I come there, I will find a life of bliss that knows no end, so I will press on.

So Mistrust and Timorous ran down the hill and Christian went on his way. Yet he thought once more of what he had heard from the men, and then he felt in his cloak for his scroll, that he might read it and find strength and peace. He felt for it but did not find it. Then Christian was in great grief and did not know what to do for the want of that which was to be his pass to The Celestial City.

At last, he thought: "I slept in the cave by the side of the hill." So he fell down on his knees to pray that God would give him grace; and then went back to look for his scroll. But as he went, what tongue could tell the grief of Christian's heart? "Oh, fool that I am!" he said, "to sleep in the daytime, so to give way to the flesh and use for

TIMOROUS

ease that rest which the Lord of the hill had made for the help of the soul."

Then, with tears and sighs, he went back, and with much care looked on this side and on that for his scroll. At length he came near to the cave where he had sat and slept. "How far," thought Christian, "have I gone in vain! Such was the lot of the Jews for their sin; they were sent back by the way of the Red Sea; and I am made to tread those steps with grief which I might have trod with joy, had it not been for this sleep. How far might I have been on my way by this time! I am made to tread those steps three times which I should have trod but once. Now I might be lost in the night, for the day is well spent. Oh, that I had not slept."

Now, by this time he had come to the cave once more, where for a while he sat down and wept; but at

Christian finds his scroll. last, as he cast a sad glance at the foot of the bench, he saw his scroll, which he caught up with haste, and put in his cloak. Words are too weak to tell the joy of Christian when he had found his scroll. He laid it up in the breast of his coat and gave thanks to God. With what a light step did he now climb the hill! But when he reached the top, the sun went down, and he soon saw that two wild beasts stood in his way. "Ah," he thought, "these beasts move in the night for their prey; and if they should meet with me in the dark, how should I fly from them? I see now the cause of all those fears that drove Mistrust

and Timorous back."

Still Christian went on, and while he thought on this, he cast up his eyes and saw a great house in front of him, the name of which was Beautiful, and it stood just by the side of the high road. So, he made haste and went on in the hope that he could rest there for a while.

The name of the man who kept the lodge of that house was Watchful, and when he saw that Christian stopped as if he would go back, he came out to him and said: "Is thy strength so small? Fear not the two wild beasts, for they are bound by chains, and are put here to try the faith of those that have it, and to find out those that have none. Keep in the midst of the path and no harm shall come to you."

Christian gains strength against sin.

Then I saw in my dream that still he went on in great fear of the wild beasts. He heard them roar, yet they did him no harm. When he had gone by them he went on with joy, till he came and stood in front of the lodge where Watchful dwelt.

CHRISTIAN: Sir, what house is this? May I rest here for the night?

WATCHFUL: This house was built by the Lord of the Hill to help those who climb up it for a good cause. Tell me, where do you come from?

CHRISTIAN: I have come from The City of Destruction and am on my way to Mount Zion; but the day is near gone, and I would like to stay here for the night, if you please.

WATCHFUL: What is your name?

CHRISTIAN: My name is now Christian, but at first it was Graceless.

WATCHFUL: How is it you came so late? The sun is now set.

Christian then told him how he lost his scroll.

WATCHFUL: Well, I will call one that lives here, who, if she likes your talk, will let you come in, for these are the rules of the house.

So he rang a bell, at the sound of which there came out of the door a grave and fair maid, whose name was Discretion. When Watchful told her why Christian had come there, she said, "What is your name?"

"It is Christian," said he, "and I wish to rest here for the night, for I see this place was built by the Lord of the Hill, to screen those from harm who come to it."

Christian meets Prudence, Piety and Charity.

So, she gave a smile, but tears stood in her eyes, and in a short time she said, "I will call forth two or three more of our house." Then she ran to the door and brought in Prudence, Piety, and Charity, who met him and said, "Come in, blessed of the Lord; this house was built by the King of the Hill for such as you." Then Christian bent down his head and went with them to the house.

PIETY: Come, good Christian, since our love prompts us to take you in to rest, let us talk with you of all that you have seen on your way.

CHRISTIAN: I would be glad to share it with you.

PIETY: How did it come that you should leave your own city for this way?

CHRISTIAN: It was God who led me; for when I was under the fears of death, I did not know which way to go. But there came a man whose name is Evangelist, and he led me to The Wicket Gate, which I would not have found, and so set me in the way that led me to this house.

PRUDENCE: And please tell us what is it that makes you wish so much to go to Mount Zion?

Christian found the way to Zion.

CHRISTIAN: It is there I hope to see Him that died on the Cross for me; and there I hope to be rid of all those things that to this day grieve me. There, I am told, is no death; and there I shall dwell with such as love the Lord. For I tell you the truth: I love Him! For it was by Him that I was eased of my load, and rid of my sin. I would like to be where there is no more death, and with those that shall cry, "Holy, holy, holy."

CHARITY: Have you a wife and babes?

CHRISTIAN: Yes, I have a wife and four young ones.

CHARITY: And why did you not bring them with you?

Christian then wept and said, "Oh, I would have been so glad to do so, but they would not come with me, nor have me leave them."

CHARITY: And did you pray to God to put it in their

hearts to go with you?

CHRISTIAN: Yes, and that with much warmth, for you must know how dear they are to me.

Thus they sat and talked till the time it was to eat. Now the table was filled with fat things and fine wine; and their talk at the table was of the Lord of the hill. They spoke of how He had fought with and slain him who had the reign of death, but with great pain to His own self, which made them love Him all the more. "For, as they said, and as I believed," said Christian, "He did it with the loss of much blood. But that which put grace in all He did, was that He did it out of a pure love to those that are His."

So Christian talked with these new friends till it grew dark, and then he took his rest in a large room, the name of which was Peace. There he slept till break of day, and then he sang a hymn.

In the morn they rose and told Christian that he should not leave till they had shown him all the rare things that were in that place. *Christian views the Lord's Armory.* They took him to the Armory, where they showed him all kinds of things, which the Lord gave for all who seek truth like him; such as sword, shield, head-piece, breast-plate, all-prayer, and shoes that would not wear out.

There he saw the rod of Moses, the nail with which Jael slew Sisera, the lamps with which Gideon put to flight the host of Midian, and the ox goad with which Shamgar slew his foes. And they brought out the jaw bone with which Samson did such great feats, and the sling and stone with which David slew Goliath of Gath, and the sword with which the Lord will kill the man of sin, in that last day when he shall rise up.

Then I saw in my dream that Christian rose to take his leave of Discretion, and of Prudence, Piety, and Charity, but they said that he must stay till the next day, that they might show him The Delectable Mountains. So they took him to the top of the house and asked him look to the South, which he did; and then a great way off, he saw a rich land, full of hills, woods, vines, shrubs, springs, and streams.

"What is the name of this land?" asked Christian.

Then they told him it was Immanuel's Land. And they said it is as much meant for you, and the like of you, as this hill is; and when you reach the place, there you may see the gate of The Celestial City. Then they gave him a sword *Christian goes on with sword drawn.* and shield, and put on him a coat of mail, which armed him from head to foot, lest he should meet some foe in the way; and they went with him down the hill.

"It is true that it is as great a toil to come down the hill as it was to go up," said Christian.

PRUDENCE: So it is, for it is a hard thing for a man to go down to The Valley of Humiliation, as you do now. For this cause we have come with you to the foot of the hill.

So, though he went down with great care, yet he caught a slip or two.

Stage Four

hen in my dream I saw that when they had come to the foot of the hill, these good friends of Christian's gave him a loaf of bread, a flask of wine, and a bunch of dry grapes. Then they left him to go on his way.

But now in this Valley of Humiliation poor Christian was hard pressed, for he had not gone far when he spied a foul fiend come in the field to meet him, whose name was Apollyon. Then did Christian fear, and he wrest in his mind if he would go back or stand his ground. But Christian thought that as he had no coat of mail on his back, to turn round might give Apollyon a chance to pierce him with his darts. So he stood his ground and turned to face his foe.

Christian meets Apollyon.

He went on, and Apollyon met him with looks of scorn.

APOLLYON: Why have you come, and to what place do you seek?

CHRISTIAN: I come from The City of Destruction, which is the place of all sin, and I am on my way to Zion.

CHRISTIAN FIGHTS APOLLYON

APOLLYON: By this I see you are mine, for of all that land I am the Prince. How is it then, that you have left your king? If I did not have a strong hope that you may do me more good, I would strike you to the ground right now with one blow.

CHRISTIAN: I was born in your realm, it is true, but you drove us too hard, and your wage was such as no man could live on.

APOLLYON: No prince likes to lose his men, nor will I as yet lose you, so I will see that you come back. What my realm yields I will give you.

CHRISTIAN: But I am bound by vows to the King of Kings; and how can I then go back with you?

APOLLYON: You have made a change, it seems, from bad to worse; but why not leave Him, and come back with me? Do this and all shall be well.

CHRISTIAN: I gave Him my faith, and swore to be true to Him. How can I go back from this?

APOLLYON: You did the same to me, and yet I will pass by all, if you will but turn and go back.

CHRISTIAN: What I gave to you, I did in my youth; but I count that the Prince under whom I now stand is able to free me of my sin. Besides, you are one full of hate; to speak truth, I like His wages better than yours. I am His and I will follow Him.

APOLLYON: You have already failed Him, and how do you now come to think you will see His wages?

Apollyon rails Christian for his sin.

CHRISTIAN: This is true, yet the Prince whom I now serve is full of love, grace, and truth towards those who turn to Him.

Then, when Apollyon saw that Christian would stand fast to his Prince, he broke out in a great rage and said, "I hate that Prince, and I hate his laws, and I have come out to stop you!"

CHRISTIAN: Take heed what you do. I am on the King's road to Zion.

Then Apollyon blocked the whole breadth of the way and said, "I am void of fear, for I swear by my wicked den that you shall not go on. Here on this spot I will put you to death."

With that he threw a dart of fire at his breast, but Christian had a shield on his arm, with which he fought it. Then did Christian draw his sword, for he saw it was time to fight. Apollyon moved fast at him and threw darts as thick as hail, with which, in spite of all that Christian could do, Apollyon gave him wounds in his head, hand, and foot.

This made Christian pause in the fight, and draw back for a time; but Apollyon still came on, and Christian once more took heart. They fought for half a day, till Christian was weak from his wounds. When Apollyon saw this, he threw him down with great force. Christian's sword fell out of his hand. Then said Apollyon, "I am sure that you are now mine!" And with that he near pressed him to death, so that Christian lost some hope.

But while he strove to make an end of Christian, that good man put out his hand in haste to feel for his sword and caught it. "Boast not, O Apollyon!" he said, and with that he struck him a blow which made his foe reel back as one that had his last wound. Then he spread out his wings and fled, so that Christian for a time saw him no more.

Christian wins his fight with Apollyon.

Then there came to him a Hand which held someleaves from the Tree of Life. Some of them Christian took, and as soon as he had put them to his wounds, he saw them heal.

Now near this place was the Valley of the Shadow of Death, and Christian knew he must go through it to get to The Celestial City. It was a land of drought and full of pits, a land that none but such as Christian could pass through, and where no man dwelt. So that here he was put more to the test than in his fight with the foul fiend, Apollyon.

As he drew near the Shadow of Death he met with two men to whom Christian then spoke:

"To what place do you go?"

MEN: Back! Back! and we would have you do the same if you prize life and peace.

CHRISTIAN: But why?

MEN: We went on as far as we dare.

CHRISTIAN: What have you seen?

MEN: Seen? Why, the Valley of the Shadow of Death. But thanks be to God, we caught sight of what lay in front of us. Death spreads its wings there. In a word it is a place full of bad men, where no law dwells.

CHRISTIAN: I do not see that what you have told me is true, but this is my way to Zion.

MEN: It may be your way, but we will not choose it for ours.

So they took their leave. Christian went on, but still with his drawn sword in his hand, for fear lest he should meet once more with a foe.

I saw then in my dream that so far as this dark vale went, there was on the right hand a deep ditch—that ditch to which the blind have led the blind as long as the world has been made. And lo, on the left hand there was a quag, in which if a man falls, he will find no firm ground for his foot to stand on. The path was not wide, and so good Christian was put more to the test; for when he sought in the dark to shun the ditch on the right side, he felt he might fall in the mire on

Christian comes to the Valley of the Shadow of Death.

the left. This went on for miles,
and in the midst of the vale was a
deep pit, which I thought to be
hell. The way was so hard for
Christian; that he cried, "Lord,
please save my soul!" With this
he went on a great while, but the
flames came close to him.

The fright of this sight
weighed great on Christian, and
he stopped on the way to think of
what he must do. He first
thought to go back, but then he

thought he might be more than half way through the vale. So he pressed on, but the fiends came near, and he cried out in a loud voice, "I will walk in the strength of the Lord God"; so they drew back, and came no further.

One thing which I saw in my dream I must not leave out. It was this: Just as Christian had come to the mouth of the pit, one of those who dwelt in it stepped up to him, and in a soft tone spoke vile things to him, and took God's name in vain, which Christian thought must have come from his own mind. *Christian* This caused him great fear, more than all the *stands at the* rest had done. To think that he should take *the pit.* *mouth of* that name in vain for which he felt so deep a love, was a great grief to him.

Then he thought he heard a voice which said: "Though I walk through the Valley of the Shadow of Death, I will fear no harm, for thou art with me."

About this time the sun rose, and from the place where he stood, he could see the way filled full of snares, traps, gins, and nets. It was so full of pits, falls, and deep holes, that had it been dark, as it was when he came through the first part of the way, he would have been cast out. And so as the day broke, Christian said, "His light shines on my head, and by His light I shall go forth."

In this light, he came to the end of the vale. Now I saw in my dream that at the end lay blood, bones, ashes, and the flesh of men. While I thought what must be the cause of this scene, I spied a cave, where giant Pagan dwelt in old times, by whose power the men that lie dead before me were put to death. But Christian held his peace, and so went by, and came to no harm.

Stage Five

ow as Christian went on in the light of day, he found there was a rise in the road, which had been built so that the path might be clear to all those who were bound for Zion.

Up this road Christian went, and saw his old friend Faithful a short way off.

Christian meets up with his old friend Faithful.

Then said Christian, "Ha! My friend! You are here? Stay, and I will join you." They went on and had sweet speech of all things that came to them on the way.

CHRISTIAN: I am so glad I caught up to you. God has joined our Spirits, so that we can walk as friends on this path.

FAITHFUL: I had thought, dear friend Christian, to have been joined with you from our town, but you did get such a start on me; so I was forced to come on this way as one.

So they spoke of all that had come to pass since they last met.

"Well, friend Faithful," said Christian, "let us talk of all that we must know for now. Tell me of what you met with on the way as you came; for I know you have met with many things."

FAITHFUL: I missed the slough of which you fell, and came straight up to the gate; but I met with one whose name was Wanton, who sought to sway me to do evil with her.

Wanton seeks to take Faithful in her sin.

CHRISTIAN: But what did she do to you?

FAITHFUL: You can not think what a tongue of false praise she has. She lay hard at me to leave with her and live a life of joy and ease.

CHRISTIAN: Thank God, you were freed from her.

FAITHFUL: I know not if I am free from her.

CHRISTIAN: Why? I know you did not give in to her wants and lures.

FAITHFUL: No, not to be stained in the flesh, but I shut my eyes so as not to be dazed by her looks. Then she railed on me, so I went my way.

CHRISTIAN: Did you meet with no other pains on the way?

FAITHFUL: When I came to the foot of the hill called Difficulty, I met with a very old man who asked me who I was. I told him that I was a Pilgrim and on my way to The Celestial City. He then asked me to dwell with him and he would pay me a fair wage. I then asked him his name and where he dwelt.

Adam the First falls on Faithful.

He said his name was Adam the First and he dwelt in the town of Deceit. I asked him about his work and his wage. He told me his work was of fine things of the world; and his wage was that I should be

PRIDE   ARROGANCY   SELF-CONCEIT   WORLDLY GLORY

his heir in the end. I then asked of his heirs by blood,
and he said he had three: Lust of the Flesh, Lust of the
Eyes, and the Pride of Life; and that I may be joined to
them for life, if I so chose.

CHRISTIAN: Well, what did you do?

FAITHFUL: Why, at first I thought I might go with
him, for I found him to be quite fair; but then it came
to my mind that he spoke false words, and when he
got me home I would be sold as a slave. So I went on
my way up the hill. Now, when I was half way up, I
looked down the hill and saw one who was after me,
swift as the wind. So he caught me and struck me
with a blow. He knocked me down, and left me for
dead. When I came up, I asked him why he beat me,

and he said he knew my heart leaned to Adam the First. And then he struck a blow and beat me down; so I lay at his feet as near dead. He would have made an end of me, but One came by and forced him to leave.

CHRISTIAN: Who was he?

FAITHFUL: I did not know at first, but as we went I saw the holes in his hands and side; and then I knew it was our Lord.

CHRISTIAN: That man who took you and beat you was Moses. He spares none who break his Law.

FAITHFUL: I also met with Discontent, who urged me to go back with him. He told me if I went the way of the Valley of Humiliation, all my friends, Pride, Arrogancy, Self-conceit, and Worldly Glory, would fear.

Discontent would have Faithful turn back.

CHRISTIAN: Well, what did you say to him?

FAITHFUL: I told him that all these he named might be called my friends, but that was when I was in the flesh; since I am now a Pilgrim of the King, they have no claim to me.

Now, I saw in my dream that as they went on, Faithful, as he chanced to look on one side, saw a man whose name was Talkative, who walked a short way off from them.

FAITHFUL: Friend, are you on your way to The Celestial City?

TALKATIVE: Yes, I am on my way there.

FAITHFUL: That is well; then I hope we might have

TALKATIVE JOINS CHRISTIAN AND FAITHFUL ON THE WAY

you join us on our way.

TALKATIVE: Very well, I will walk with you.

FAITHFUL: Come then, let us speak of those things that are good for our souls.

TALKATIVE: I am glad to have met with those who speak the truth, there are but few who care so to spend their time.

FAITHFUL: And what can be of such good use of the tongue and mouth of men on earth than to speak of the things of God and the world to come!

TALKATIVE: That is well said; and I will add—if a man does love to talk of the things of God, where shall he find things penned so sweet as in His Word? For to talk of such things a man may know much of this vain world and the joy of things above.

FAITHFUL: I am glad to hear these things from you.

TALKATIVE: Alas! The want of this is the cause that so many are blind to the need of faith and the work of grace in their soul. They would live bound by the works of the law, by which no man can see God's rest.

FAITHFUL: But, all of this is the gift of God; no man can come to them by his own skill, or by talk of them.

TALKATIVE: All this I know well, for a man can not see this. It comes from the grace of God.

All the while, Christian was a few steps back and said to Faithful, "This man with whom you speak will, with his tongue, trick them that do not know him."

FAITHFUL: Do you know him then? Pray, who is he?

CHRISTIAN: He is Talkative: he dwells in our town. He is the son of Say-well. This man is for any talk. As he talks now with you, so he will talk with those who do not know our King. The more drink he has in his crown, the more of these things he has in his mouth. Truth has no place in his heart or his speech; all he has lies in his tongue and his way is to make noise. He thinks that if he hears and says what is right it will make him a good Christian, but talk does not prove that good fruit is in his heart and life.

Talkative does not do as he speaks.

FAITHFUL: Well then, how shall we be rid of him?

CHRISTIAN: Take my advice and do as I ask you and you shall find that he will soon be sick of you too, except God touch his heart and turn it.

So Christian sent Faithful to speak with Talkative of the deep things of God and faith, and asked him if these truths be in his heart.

FAITHFUL: So, my friend, how is the grace of God found when it is in the heart of a man?

TALKATIVE: You ask well. Where the grace of God is in the heart, it causes there to be a cry from one's sin.

> To cry out from sin is no sign of grace.

FAITHFUL: You mean, it leads the soul to hate sin.

TALKATIVE: Why, is not a cry from sin the same as hate of sin?

FAITHFUL: No, they are a great deal at odds. What a man knows is no sign of grace, but what is from the heart is a sign of grace in the soul.

TALKATIVE: This kind of talk does not feel good.

FAITHFUL: Well, your faith is in word and tongue, not in deed and truth.

TALKATIVE: Since you are so apt to judge me, I say you are a sad man and not fit to talk with; and so I will now take my leave of you.

Then came up Christian to Faithful and said, "Did I not tell you how it would go? Your words and his lusts will not agree. It is best that he has left us."

FAITHFUL: But I am glad we had this talk. It may be that he may think of it from time to time and turn.

Stage Six

n the course of time the road they took brought them to a town, the name of which is Vanity, where there is a fair kept through the whole year, called Vanity Fair, and all that is bought or sold there is vain and void of worth. At all times, there are to be seen cheats, games, plays, fools, knaves, and rogues, of every kind. Here too can be found rows and streets where the sales of the fair can be found. Yet he that will go to The Celestial City must pass through this fair.

As soon as Christian and Faithful came to the town, a crowd drew round them and some said they had lost their wits, to dress and speak as they did, and to set no store by the choice goods for sale in Vanity Fair. They were asked by men in the town, "What will you buy?" But they looked at them and said, "We buy the truth!" When Christian spoke, his words drew from these folks fierce taunts and jeers, and soon the noise and stir grew to such a height that the chief man of the fair sent his friends to seize these two strange men, and he urged them to tell him from where they came, and why they wore such strange clothes.

Christian and Faithful told them the truth from their heart, but those who sat to judge the case thought that they must be mad, or else they had come to stir up strife at the fair; so they beat them with

Christian and Faithful brought to court in the town.

sticks, and put them in a cage, that they might be a sight for all the men at the fair. Then the worse sort of folk sought to taunt them, out of spite, and some threw things at them for mere sport; but Christian and Faithful gave good words for bad, and bore all in such a meek way, that not a few took their part. This led to blows and fights, and the blame was laid on Christian and Faithful, who were then made to toil up and down the fair in chains, till, faint with stripes, they were at length set with their feet in the stocks. But they bore their griefs and woes with joy, for they saw in them the pledge from their King that all should be well in the end.

Then a court sat to try them. The name of the Judge was Lord Hate-Good; and the crime laid to their charge was that they had come to Vanity Fair to spoil its trade, and stir up strife in the town; and had won not a few men to their side, in spite of the law of the prince of the place.

Faithful said to the Judge, "I am a man of peace, but I did wage war on Sin. As for the prince they speak of, since he is Beelzebub, the foe of our Lord, I hold him and all his host in scorn."

Those who took Faithful's part were won by the force of plain truth in his words; but the judge said, "Let those speak who know this man." So three men, whose names were Envy, Superstition, and Pick-thank, stood forth and swore to speak the truth, and tell what they knew of Faithful. Envy said, "My lord, this man cares not for kings or laws, but seeks to spread his own views, and to teach men what he calls faith. I heard him say that the ways of our town of Vanity are vile. And does he not in all this speak ill of us?"

Then Superstition said, "My lord, I know not much of this man, and have no wish to know

ENVY

LORD HATE-GOOD

more; but of this I am sure, that he is a bad man, for he says that our creeds are vain."

Pick-thank was then bid to say what he knew, and he said: "My lord, I have known this man for a long time, and have heard him say things that ought not to be said. He rails at our great Prince Beelzebub, and says that if all men were like him, that our prince should no more hold sway. More than this, he has been heard to rail on you, my lord, who is now his judge."

Then said the Judge to Faithful: "You base man! Have you heard what these good folk have said of you?"

FAITHFUL: May I speak a few words in my own cause?

JUDGE: Your just doom would be to die on the spot; still, let us hear what you have to say.

FAITHFUL: To Mr. Envy I say, that all laws and modes of life in which men hear not the Word of God are full of sin. As to the charge of Mr. Superstition, I would urge that we can not be saved if we do not the will of God. To Mr. Pick-thank, I say that men should flee from the Prince of this town and his friends, as from the wrath to come. And so, I pray the Lord to help me.

Then the Judge, to sum up the case, spoke thus: "You see this man who has made such a stir in our town. You have heard what these good men have said of him, which he owns to be true. It rests now with you to save his life or hang him."

The twelve men who had Faithful's life in their hands spoke in a low tone: "This man is full of

SUPERSTITION

schisms," said Mr. Blindman. "Out of the world with him," said Mr. Nogood.

"I hate the mere sight of him," said Mr. Malice.

"From the first I could not bear him," said Mr. Love-ease.

"Nor I, for he would be sure to blame my ways," said Mr. Live-loose.

"Hang him, hang him!" said Mr. Heady.

"A low wretch," said Mr. High-mind.

"I long to crush him," said Mr. Enmity.

"He is a rogue," said Mr. Liar.

"Death is too good for him," said Mr. Cruelty.

"Let us kill him, that he may be out of the way," said Mr. Hate-light.

Then said Mr. Implacable: "Not to gain all the world would I make peace with him, so let us doom him to death." And so they did, and in a short time he was led back to the place from where he came, there to be put to the worst death that could be thought of. They brought him out as was their law, and scourged him, then they beat him, then they lanced his flesh with knives, and then stoned him and pricked him with their swords; and at last they burned him to ashes at the stake. Thus Faithful came to his end.

Faithful judged and met with a cruel death.

Now I saw that there stood near the crowd a strange car with two bright steeds, which, as soon as his foes had slain him, took Faithful up through the clouds straight to The Celestial City, with the sound of the

harp and lute.

As for Christian, he was sent back to the cage for some time. But He who rules all things brought it to pass, by the hands of those who were changed in heart, for Christian to be freed.

Stage Seven

ow I saw in my dream that Christian went forth and there came to join him one named Hopeful, who did so from what he had heard and seen of Christian and Faithful at the fair. So, while one lost his life for the truth, a new man rose from the throng at the fair to tread the same way with Christian. And Hopeful said there were more men of the fair who would take their turn to come as well.

Christian is joined by Hopeful.

Then Christian and Hopeful came to a hill called Lucre, where stood Demas to call men to a mine of great wealth.

"Ho, turn here and I will show you a grand thing." said Demas.

CHRISTIAN: What is so grand that we should turn out of the way?

DEMAS: If you come to this mine, you can be rich.

HOPEFUL: Let us go and see.

CHRISTIAN: Not I. I have heard of this place and how many there have been slain. That wealth is a snare to those that seek it.

Then Christian said to Hopeful, "Let us not yield,

but still keep on our way."

Then Demas said, "But will you not first come here and see?"

Then Christian spoke, "Demas, you are a foe to the right ways of the Lord of this road and doomed for your own false ways. Will you bring us in to tread the path of death?"

Thus they left Demas and went their way.

By and by their way lay just on the bank of a pure stream, from which they drank. On each side of it were green trees that bore fruit, and in a field through which it ran they lay down to sleep. When they woke up they sat for a while in the shade of the boughs. Thus they went on for three or four days, and to pass the time they sang:

"He that can tell
What sweet fresh fruit, yea leaves
these trees do yield,
Will soon sell all, that he may
buy this field."

Now I saw in my dream that they had not gone far when the path was rough and their feet sore. Yet, on the left hand of the road was By-path Meadow, a fair green field with a smooth path through it, and a stile. "Come, good Hopeful," said Christian, "let us walk on the grass."

HOPEFUL: But what if this path should lead us the

wrong way?

CHRISTIAN: How can it? Look, does it not go by the way side?

So they set off through the field. But they had not gone far when they saw in front of them a man, Vain-confidence by name, who told them that the path led to the gates of The Celestial City. So the man went first, but soon the night came, and it grew so dark that they lost sight of their guide, who, since he did not see the path in front of him, fell in a deep pit and was heard of no more.

The two Pilgrims leave the right path.

"Where are we now?" said Hopeful.

Christian did not speak, as he thought he had led his friend out of the way. And now light was seen to flash from the sky, and rain came down in streams.

HOPEFUL: (with a groan) Oh, I wish that we had kept on the right way!

CHRISTIAN: Who could have thought that this path should lead us wrong?

HOPEFUL: I had my fears from the first and said so when we steered this way.

CHRISTIAN: Good friend, I grieve that I have brought you out of the right path.

HOPEFUL: Say no more, no doubt it is for our good.

CHRISTIAN: We must not stand like this. Let us try to go back.

HOPEFUL: But, good Christian, let me go first.

Then they heard a voice say, "Set your heart to the high way, and turn once more to the way you have trod." But by this time the stream was deep from the rain that fell, and to go back did not seem safe; yet they went back, though it was so dark and the stream ran so high that once or twice they felt as if they might drown. Though they used all their skill, they could not get back to the way that night. So they found a safe spot from the rain, in the boughs of a tree, and there they slept till the break of day.

Now, not far from the place where they lay was Doubting Castle. The lord of the place was Giant Despair; and it was on his ground that they now slept. There, Giant Despair found them, and with a gruff voice he woke them up.

"Who are you?" he said, "and what brought you here?" They told him that they had lost their way.

Then said Giant Despair, "You have no right to force your way in here; the ground on which you lie is mine. Now you shall pay!"

They had not much to say, as they knew that they were in fault. So Giant Despair drove them on, and put them in a dark and foul cell in a strong hold. Here

GIANT DESPAIR

they were kept for three days, and they had no light nor food, nor a drop to drink all that time, and no one to ask them how they did. Now Giant Despair had a wife, whose name was Diffidence, and he told her all he had done.

Christian and Hopeful are caught by Giant Despair.

Then he asked, "What do you think will be the best way to treat them?"

"Beat them well," said Diffidence.

So when he rose he took a stout stick from a crab tree and went down to the cell where poor Christian and Hopeful lay. He beat them as if they had been dogs, so that they could not move on the floor, for the pain was so great. They spent all that day in sighs and tears.

The next day he came once more and found them sore from their stripes, and said that since there was no chance for them to be let out of the cell, their best way would be to put an end to their own lives. "For why should you wish to live," he said, "with all this woe?" But they told him they did hope he would let them go. With that he sprang up with a fierce look, and no doubt would have made an end of them, but that he fell in one of his fits (which come upon him from time to time), and lost the use of his hand. So he drew back and left them to think of what he had said.

CHRISTIAN: Friend, what shall we do? The life that we now lead is worse than death. For my part I know not which is best, to live like this or to die. I feel that the grave would be less sad to me than this cell. Shall we let Giant Despair rule us?

HOPEFUL: It is true our case is a sad one, and to die would be more sweet to me than to live here; yet let us bear in mind that the Lord of that land to which we go has said: "Thou shalt not kill."† And by this act we kill our souls as well. My friend Christian, you talk of ease in the grave, but can a man go to bliss who takes his own life? All the law is not in the hands of Giant Despair. Who knows but it may be that God, who made the world, may cause him to die, or lose the use of his limbs as he did at first. I have made up my mind to gird up my heart and try to get us out of this mess. I have been a fool not to do so when he first came to the cell. But let us not put an end to our own lives, for a good time may come yet.

Hopeful helps Christian to not lose hope.

By these words Hopeful did change the tone of Christian's mind.

Well, at night the Giant went down to the cell to see if life was still in them, and in truth, that life was in them was all that could be said, for from their wounds and want of food they did no more than just breathe. When Giant Despair found they were not dead, he fell in a great rage, and said that it should be worse with them than if they had not been born. At this they shook with fear, and Christian fell down faint. When he came to, Hopeful said: "My friend, call to mind how strong in faith you have been till now. Say, could Apollyon hurt you, or all that you heard, or saw, or felt

† EXOD. 20:13

in the Valley of the Shadow of Death? Look at the fears, the griefs, the woes that you have gone through. And now are you to be cast down! I, too, am in this cell, far more weak a man than you, and Giant Despair dealt his blows at me as well as you, and keeps me from food and light. Let us both (if but to shun the shame) bear up as well as we can."

When night came on, the wife of Giant Despair said to him, "Well, will the two men yield?"

To which he said, "No. They choose to stand firm, and will not put an end to their lives."

Then said Diffidence, "At dawn of day take them to the yard, and show them the graves and bones where all those whom you have put to death have been thrown, and make use of threats this time."

So in the morn, Giant Despair took them to this place, and said, "In ten days time you shall be thrown in here if you do not yield."

"Go, get down to your den once more." With that he beat them all the way back, and there they lay the whole day in pain.

Now, when night was come, Diffidence said to Giant Despair, "I fear much that these men live on in hopes to pick the lock of the cell and get free."

"So you say, my dear?" said Giant Despair to his wife, "then at sun rise I will search them."

Now, on that night, as Christian and Hopeful lay in the den, they fell on their knees to pray, and knelt till the day broke. Then Christian jumped up and said:

CHRISTIAN AND HOPEFUL ESCAPE FROM GIANT DESPAIR

"Fool that I am to lie in this dark den when I might walk at large! I have a key in my pouch, the name of which is Promise, that I feel sure will turn the lock of all the doors in Doubting Castle."

Then said Hopeful, "That is good news; take it from your cloak, and let us try it."

So Christian put it in the lock, and when the bolt sprang back, the door flew wide, and Christian and Hopeful both came out. When they got to the yard door the key did just as well; but the lock of the last strong gate of Doubting Castle went hard, yet it did turn at last. The hinge gave so loud a creak that it woke up Giant Despair, who rose to search for the two men.

But just then he fell in to one of his fits and his limbs fell, so that he could by no means catch them. Christian and Hopeful now fled back to the high way, and were safe out of his grounds. When they sat down to rest on a stile, they said they would warn those who might come by on this road. So they carved these words on a post: "This the way to Doubting Castle, which is kept by Giant Despair, who loves not the King of The Celestial City, and seeks to kill all who would go there."

Stage Eight

hen they came to The Delectable Mountains, which the Lord of the Hill owns. Here they saw fruit trees, vines, shrubs, woods, and streams, and drank and ate of the grapes. Now there were men at the tops of these hills who kept watch on their flocks, and as they stood by the road, Christian and Hopeful leaned on their staffs to rest, and they spoke to the men: "Who owns these Delectable Mountains, and whose are the sheep that feed on them?"

MEN: These hills are Immanuel's, and the sheep are His too, and He laid down his life for them.

CHRISTIAN: Is this the way to The Celestial City?

MEN: You are on the right road.

CHRISTIAN: How far is it?

MEN: Too far for all but those that shall get there in good truth.

CHRISTIAN: Is the way safe?

MEN: Safe for those for whom it is to be safe, but the men of sin shall fall there.

CHRISTIAN: Is there a place of rest here for those that faint on the road?

MEN: The Lord of these Hills gave us a charge to help those that came here, should they be known to us or not; so the good things of the place are yours.

I then saw in my dream that the men said, "Why have you come, and by what means have you got so far? For but few of those that set out come here to show their face on these hills."

So when Christian and Hopeful told their tale, the men cast a kind glance at them, and said, "With joy we greet you on The Delectable Mountains!"

Their names were Knowledge, Experience, Watchful, and Sincere, and they led Christian and Hopeful by the hand to their tents, and gave them food to eat, and they soon went to sleep for the night.

When the morn broke, the men woke up Christian and Hopeful, and took them to a spot where they saw a bright view on all sides. Then they went with them *The mount of Error.* to the top of a high hill, the name of which was Error; it was steep on the far off side, and they urged them to look down at the foot of it. So Christian and Hopeful cast their eyes down and saw there some men who had lost their lives by a fall from the top (men who had been made to err, for they had put their trust in false guides).

"Have you not heard of them?" said the men.

CHRISTIAN: Yes, I have.

MEN: These are they, and to this day they have not been put in a tomb, but are left here to warn men to take care how they come too near the edge of this hill.

GIANT DESPAIR SENT THEM OUT QUITE BLIND

Then I saw that they had led them to the top of
Mount Caution and asked them to look far off from
that stile, and they said, "There goes a path to
Doubting Castle, which is kept by Giant Despair. The
men whom you see there came as you do now, till they

got up to that stile. Since the right way was rough to walk in, they chose to go through a field, and there Giant Despair took them, and shut them up in Doubting Castle, where they were kept in a cell for a while. At last sent them out quite blind, and there they are still. At this Christian gave a look at Hopeful, and they both burst out with sobs and tears, but yet said not a word.

Then the four men took them up a high hill, the name of which was Clear, that they might see the gates of The Celestial City, with the aid of a glass to look through; but their hands shook, so they could not see it well.

When Christian and Hopeful thought they would move on, one of the men gave them a note for the way; the next bid them to watch out for the Flatterer; then Experience warned them to take heed that they sleep not on The Enchanted Ground; and the fourth sent them Godspeed. Now it was that I woke from my dream.

Stage Nine

hen I slept, and dreamt once more, and saw Christian and Hopeful go down near the foot of these hills where lies the land of Conceit, which joins the way to Mount Zion, by a small lane. Here they met a brisk lad, whose name was Ignorance, to whom Christian said; "Where have you come from, and to what place do you go?" Ignorance comes out of the land of Conceit.

IGNORANCE: Sir, I was born in the land that lies off there on the left, and I wish to go to The Celestial City.

CHRISTIAN: How do you think to get in at the gate?

IGNORANCE: Just as the rest of the world does.

CHRISTIAN: But what have you to show at that gate so that you may pass through it?

IGNORANCE: I know my Lord's will, and I have led a good life. I pay for all that I have, I give tithes, and give alms, and have left my own land for that to which I now go.

CHRISTIAN: But you did not come in at the gate that is at the head of this way. You came in through a small lane; so that I fear, though you may think well of all you have done, that when the time shall come, you will have this laid to your charge, that you are a thief and so you will not get in.

IGNORANCE: Well, I do not know you. You keep to your own creed, and I will keep to mine, and I hope all will be well. And as for the gate that you talk of, all the world knows that it is far from our land, and I do not think that there is a man in all our parts who knows the way to it. I do not see what need there is that he should, since we have, as you see, a fine green lane at the next turn that comes down from our part of the world.

Christian said in a low tone of voice to Hopeful, "There is more hope for a fool than for him."

IGNORANCE

HOPEFUL: Let us pass on if you will, and talk to him now and then, when he can bear it.

So as they went on, Christian told his friend of one called Little-Faith, a good man, who dwelt in the town of Sincere. Little-Faith had gone on a long trip, as we do now, sought to sit and sleep for a short time, but it came that three strong rogues, Faint-heart, Mistrust, and Guilt, spied Little-Faith where he was and came up to him with speed. Just as he awoke, they bid him to stand and hand to them his purse. But Little-Faith feared to lose his wealth, so Mistrust ran up to him and pulled his bag of gold from his hands. Then he cried out, "Thieves,

Christian tells the story of Little-Faith.

thieves!" Then Guilt, with a great club in his hand, struck Little-Faith on the head, and with that blow he fell flat to the ground; where he lay as one that would bleed to death. Now the thieves took to their heels, so they would not have to face Great-Grace, from the town of Good-Confidence. Soon Little-Faith came to his wits, and made on his way.

HOPEFUL: Did they get all that he had?

CHRISTIAN: No, they did not find the place where

GREAT-GRACE

his jewels were hid; but since they stole his loose change, he was forced to beg the rest of his way.

HOPEFUL: Poor man! This must have been a great grief to him.

CHRISTIAN: Grief! What a grief it was. I was told he was mixed up all the rest of the way, and told the tale of his woes to all he met.

HOPEFUL: Well, the three thieves were full of shame and fear, for sure.

CHRISTIAN: True, they have fled many times, when the King's Champion, Great-Grace had come. Like Little-Faith, not all can be a Champion of the King. Some are strong, some are weak; some have great faith, some have little faith; that is why Little-Faith fell as he did.

HOPEFUL: I would have wished Great-Grace would have come for his sake.

CHRISTIAN: The battle would have been fierce, and Great-Grace would have had his hands full, no doubt, but he would have the King's strength.†

HOPEFUL: What must one do when robbed on the King's high way?

CHRISTIAN: There are two things: First, be sure to take the shield of faith, to quench the darts of foes.†† Second, be sure to take one of the King's own to help in times of need.

So they went on, and Ignorance walked in their steps a short way from them, till they saw a road branch off from the one they were in, and they did not

† ACTS 4:33 †† EPH. 6:16

know which of the two to take.

As they stood to think of it, a man whose skin was black, but who was clad in a white robe, came to them and said, "Why do you stand here?" They told him that they were on their way to The Celestial City, but knew not which of the two roads to take.

"Come with me, then," said the man, "for it is there that I mean to go."

So they went with him, though it was clear that the road must have made a bend, for they soon found their backs were turned on The Celestial City.

In a short while, Christian and Hopeful were both caught in a net, and did not know what to do; and with that the white robe fell off the man's back. Then they saw where they were. So there they sat down and wept, for they could not be freed.

CHRISTIAN: Did not one of the four men who kept guard on their sheep tell us to take care lest Flatterer should spread out a net for our feet?

The Pilgrims caught in a net by the Flatterer.

HOPEFUL: Those men, too, gave us a note to keep in the way, but we have not read it, and so have not stayed on the right path.

So they laid in the net to weep and wail.

At last they saw a Bright One come up to them with a whip of fine cords in his hand, who said, "Why are you here? And from where do you come?"

They told him that their wish was to go to Zion, but that they had been led out of the way by a bad man with a white cloak on, who said he was bound for the same place, and he would show them the road.

Then he said, "It is Flatterer, a false man, who has put on the garb of a Bright One for a time."

So he tore the net and let the men out. Then he told them to come with him, that he might set them in the right way once more. He said to them, "Where were you last night?"

"With the men who kept watch on their sheep on The Delectable Mountains."

Then he said, "But when you stood before this false man, why did you not read your note?"

They told him they had not thought of it.

Now I saw in my dream that he made them to lie down, and whipped them sore, to teach them the good way in which they should walk; and he said, "Those whom I love I scold."†

So they gave him thanks for what he had taught them, and went on the right way up the hill with a song of joy.

Now, while they strode on, they saw one a far off who came on the way to meet them. Then Christian said to his friend, "Look, a man comes with his back to Zion, and he comes to meet us."

HOPEFUL: I see him. Let us take care, lest he should prove to be a Flatterer.

So he drew near and met them. His name was Athiest, and he asked why they walked on so.

"We are on our way to Mt. Zion," said Christian.

† PROV. 3:12a

ATHIEST

Then Athiest fell in to a great laugh.

"Why do you laugh?" asked Christian.

ATHIEST: I laugh to see what fools you are to go on such a trip, and find such pain.

CHRISTIAN: Why, do you think we shall not find it?

ATHIEST: Find it! There is no such place as you dream of in all this world.

CHRISTIAN: But there is in the world to come.

ATHIEST: When I was at home in my own land I heard as you now speak, and went out to see, and I have sought this Zion for one score years, but find no more of it than the first day I set out.

Athiest proves he is a fool.

CHRISTIAN: We have both heard and know that such a place is to be found.

ATHIEST: I once thought the same, but now I go back and seek the things I cast off for hopes of that which I now see is not real.

Then Hopeful said to Christian, "Take heed, he is one of the Flatterers. Are we not to walk by faith?"†

So they turned from the man, and he laughed more at them, and went his way.

At length they came to a land where the air made men sleep, and here the lids of Hopeful's eyes dropped, and he said, "Let us lie down here and take a nap."

They come to the Enchanted Ground.

CHRISTIAN: By no means! If we sleep now we will wake no more.

HOPEFUL: Nay, friend Christian, sleep is sweet to the man who has spent the day in toil.

† 2 COR. 5:7

CHRISTIAN: Do you not call to mind that one of the men who kept watch on the sheep urged us to take care and watch for The Enchanted Ground? He meant that we should take heed not to sleep; so let us not sleep, but watch!

Christian and Hopeful talk to not sleep.

HOPEFUL: I see I am in fault.

CHRISTIAN: Now then, to keep sleep from our eyes I will ask you, as we go, to tell me how you came at first to do as you do now ?

HOPEFUL: Do you mean how I first came to look towards the good of my soul?

CHRISTIAN: Yes.

HOPEFUL: For a long time the things that were seen and sold at Vanity Fair were a great joy to me.

CHRISTIAN: What things do you speak of?

HOPEFUL: All the goods of this life; such as lies, oaths, drink; in a word, love of self and all that tends to kill the soul. But I heard from you and Faithful that the end of these things is death.†

CHRISTIAN: And did you know of your own sin?

HOPEFUL: No, I shut my eyes to sin and the light of God's Word.

CHRISTIAN: Then what was the cause of the first work of God's Spirit upon you?

HOPEFUL: Well, first I was blind to the fact that this was the work of God on me. Then, sin was still yet sweet to my flesh, and I loathed to leave it. Third, I could not tell how to part with my old friends. Fourth, I could not bear the hours in which my sin

† ROM. 6:21-23

weighed down on my heart. I thought I must change my life, or I would be damned.

CHRISTIAN: And how did your life change?

HOPEFUL: I fled from, not only my sin, by my sinful friends, and took up to pray, read God's Word, weep for sin, and speak truth to my friends.

CHRISTIAN: And did you think you were well then?

HOPEFUL: Yes, for a while, but the Word was brought to me which said, "By the works of the law shall no flesh be just,"† and "there are none who seek God, no not one."††

CHRISTIAN: And then what did you do?

HOPEFUL: Do? I broke my mind to Faithful, for we were friends. And he told me that I must be a man that could not ever sin, or else the good in all the world could not save me.

CHRISTIAN: And did you think he spoke truth?

HOPEFUL: He told me this when I was still in my sin. I thought him to be a fool for his pains, but I now see that I am the one that erred.

CHRISTIAN: And did you think from your talk with Faithful, that there was such a man to be found to whom it might be said had no sin?

HOPEFUL: I thought it strange at first, but he told me it was the Lord Jesus Christ, that dwells on the right hand of the Most High.††† And he told me He is God, and that He died the death of the cross for me, if I trust in Him.

CHRISTIAN: And did you?

† GAL. 2:16 †† ROM. 3:11 ††† HEB. 10-12-21

HOPEFUL: I shed much tears and felt a great pain in my soul, then I came to trust in the Savior.

And so they talked as they went on their way.

THE LAND OF BEULAH

Stage Ten

ut I saw in my dream that by this time Christian and Hopeful had gone through The Enchanted Ground, and had come to the land of Beulah, where the air is sweet. Their way lay through this land, but they made no haste to leave it, for here they heard the birds sing all day long, and the sun shone day and night. The Valley of Death was on the left, and it was out of the reach of Giant Despair; nor could they so much as see Doubting Castle.

From here they were in sight of Zion, and some of the Bright Ones came to meet them. Here, too, they heard the voice of those who dwelt in Zion, and had a good view of this land of bliss, which was built of rare gems of all hues, and the streets were laid with gold. The rays of light which shone on Christian were too bright for him to bear, and he fell sick—and Hopeful had a fit of the same kind. So they laid down for a time, and wept, for their joy was too much for them to bear.

They find joy in the Land of Beulah.

At length, step by step, they drew near to Zion, and saw that the gates were flung back.

A man stood in the way, to whom Christian and Hopeful said, "Whose vines and crops are these?"

He told them they were the King's, and were put there to give joy to those who should go on the road. So he let them eat what fruit they chose, and took them to see the King's walks; where they slept.

Now I saw in my dream that they spoke more in their sleep than they had done all the rest of the way, and all I could do was laugh at this. But the man said, "Why do you laugh at it? The juice from the grapes of this vine is so sweet it can cause the lips of them that sleep to speak."

I then saw that when they woke, they yearned to go up to Zion; but as I said, the sun threw off such bright rays from The Celestial City, which was built of pure gold, that they could not look on it, but through a glass which was made for that end.

Now as they went, they met with two men in white robes, and the face of each shone bright as the light. These men said, "Where do you come from?" And when they told them, the Bright Ones said, "You have but one thing more to do, which is a hard one, and then you are in Zion."

Christian and Hopeful did then beg of the two men to go with them; which they did. But, they said, "It is by your own faith that you must gain it."

The River of Death must be crossed.

Now there lay before them a fierce stream which was broad and deep; it had no bridge, and the mere sight of it did so stun Christian and Hopeful that they could not move.

But the men who went with them said, "You can not come to the gate but through this stream."

"Is there no way but this to the gate?" said poor Christian.

"Yes, there is one," they said, "but there have been but two men, Enoch and Elijah who have trod that path since the world was made."

When Christian and Hopeful cast their eyes on the stream once more, they felt their hearts sink with fear, and gave a look this way and that in much dread of the waves. Yet through it lay the way to Zion.

"Is the stream all of one depth?" said Christian. He was told that it was not, yet since there was no help, he would find the stream more or less deep, as he had faith in the King of the place.

So they set foot on the stream, but Christian gave a loud cry to his good friend Hopeful, and said, "The waves close round my head, and I sink." Then said Hopeful, "Be of good cheer; my feet feel the bed of the stream, and it is good."

But Christian said, "Ah, Hopeful, the pains of death have got hold of me; I shall not reach the land that I long for." And with that a cloud came on his sight, so that he could not see.

Hopeful had much to do to keep Christian's head out of the stream. At times he would sink, and then in a while he would rise up half dead.

Then said Hopeful, "My friend, all this is sent to try you, if you will call to mind all that God has done for you, and trust on Him in your heart.

At these words Hopeful saw that Christian was in deep thought; so he said to him, "Be of good cheer, Christ will make you whole."

Then Christian broke out with a loud voice, "Oh, I see Him, and He speaks to me and says, 'When you pass through the deep streams, I will be with you.'"†

Through death we pass from this world to the next.
And then they both gained strength, and the stream was as still as a stone, so that Christian felt the bed of it with his feet, and he could then walk through it. So they got to the right bank, where the two men in bright robes stood to wait for them, and left their old clothes in the stream.

Now you must bear in mind that Zion was on a steep hill, but Christian and Hopeful went up with ease and great speed, for they had these two men to lead them by the arms.

The hill stood in the sky, so in sweet talk they went up through the air. The Bright Ones told them of the bliss of the place, which they said was such as no tongue could tell, and that there they would see the Tree of Life, and eat of the fruits of it.

When you come there, they said, white robes will be put on you, and your talk from day to day shall be with the King and those that are His for all time. There you shall not see such things as you saw on earth, such as care and want, and woe and death. You

† Isa. 43:2

now go to be with Abraham, Isaac, and Jacob.

"What must we do there?" asked Christian and Hopeful.

They said, "You will have rest for all your toil, and joy for all your grief. You will reap what you have sown—the fruit of all the tears you shed for the King by the way. In that place you will wear crowns of gold, and have at all times a sight of Him who sits on the throne. There you shall serve Him with love, with shouts of joy and with songs of praise."

Now, while they thus drew up to the gate, a host of saints came to meet them, to whom the two Bright Ones said, "These are men who felt love for our Lord when they were in the world, and left all for His name; and He sent us to bring them far on their way, that they might go in and look on their Lord with joy."

Then the whole host with great shouts came round on all sides (as it were to guard them); so that it would seem to Christian and Hopeful as if all Zion had come down to meet them.

Now, when Christian and Hopeful went in at the gate a great change took place in them, and they were clothed in robes that shone like gold. There were bright hosts that came with harps and crowns, and they said to them: "Come, ye, in the joy of the Lord." And then I heard all the bells in Zion ring.

Now, just as the gates were flung back for the men to pass in, I had a sight of Zion, which shone like the sun. The ground was of gold, and those who dwelt there had love in their eyes, crowns on their heads, and palms in their hands, and with one voice they sent forth shouts of praise.

But the gates were now once more shut, and I could but wish that I, too, had gone in to share this bliss. Then I woke, and lo, it was a dream.

END OF PART I

BUNYAN TALKS WITH MR. SAGACITY ABOUT CHRISTIAN'S QUEST
FOR THE CELESTIAL CITY

Part II

Stage One

nce more I had a dream, and an old man came to where I lay, so I got up, and we walked on the way. I spoke with the old man and our talk was of dear Christian and his trek.

"Sir," I said, "what town is there that lies on the left hand of our way?"

Then said Mr. Sagacity, for that was his name, "It is the City of Destruction, filled with ill folk of all sort."

"Well Sir, did you hear of one whose name was Christian, that went from that town to seek the Celestial City?"

"Hear of him! Ay, and I heard of all the frights, fears, cries, moans, and pains that he met with in the way. And when he was here all who spoke of him said he was a fool; yet now that he walks in white, with a gold chain on his neck, and wears a crown of gold, with pearls on his head, he is praised by men. Many now yearn for his gains, yet will not seek to run his course," said Mr. Sagacity.

"I dare say," I said, "I am glad, for his poor sake, that he is now at rest from all his toil, and now he reaps the fruit of his tears with joy. But pray sir, while it is fresh in my mind, what do you hear of his wife and babes?"

SAGACITY: Christiana and her sons? They plan to do as Christian did; for though they all played the fool at first, yet they have packed up and gone in his ways. Since you and I are to speak of this for quite some time, I will tell you the whole tale.

Christiana, the wife of Christian, had been on her knees to pray, and as she rose, she heard a loud knock at the door. "If you come in God's name," she said, "come in." Then a form, dressed in robes as white as snow, threw back the door, and said: "Peace be to this house." At this great sight, Christiana at first grew pale with fear, but in a short time took heart and told him she would like to know where he came from, and why. So he said his name was Secret, and that he dwelt with those that are on high.

SECRET: Christiana, here is a note for you, which I have brought from your dear Christian."

CHRISTIANA REPENTS

So she took it, broke the seal, and read these words, which were in gold:

"To my dear wife. The King would have you do as I have done, for it is the way to come to His land, and to dwell with Him in joy."

When Christiana read this, she shed tears, and said to him who brought the note: "Sir, will you take me and my sons with you, that we may bow down to this King?" But he said: "Christiana, joy is born of grief: care must come first, then bliss. To reach the land where I dwell you must go through toils, as well as scorn and taunts. But take the road that leads up to the field gate which stands in the head of the way; and I wish you all good speed. Please wear this note in your breast, that you may read it on the way till it has sunk in your heart, but you must give it up at the last gate that leads to The Celestial City."

Christiana pleads for her and her sons.

Then Christiana spoke to her boys, and said: "My sons, I have of late been sad at the death of Christian, your dear dad. But I feel sure now that it is well with him, and that he dwells in the land of life and peace. I have felt deep grief at the thoughts of the state of my own soul as well as yours; for we were wrong to let our hearts grow cold, and turn a deaf ear to him in the time of his woe, and hold back from him when he fled from this City of Destruction.

The thought of these things would kill me, were it not for a dream which I had last night, and for what a guest who came here at dawn has told me. So come,

CHRISTIANA SPEAKS TO HER KIN

my dear ones, let us make our way at once to the gate that leads to The Celestial City, that we may see your dad and be there with him and his friends."

Then her first two sons burst out in tears of joy that Christiana's heart was set that way.

Now while they put all things right that they might go, two friends of Christiana's came up to her house, and knocked at the door. To them she said: "If you come in God's name, come in." Her speech seemed strange to them. Yet they came in and said: "Pray what do you mean by this?"

Timorous and Mercy come to see Christiana.

"I mean to leave my home," she said to Mrs. Timorous, for that was the name of one of her friends.

TIMOROUS: To what end, please tell me?

CHRISTIANA: To go to my dear Christian.

And with that she wept.

TIMOROUS: Can it be so? Who or what has brought you to this state of mind?

CHRISTIANA: Oh! my friend, if you did but know as much as I do, you would be glad to go with me.

TIMOROUS: Pray what new tale have you got hold of that draws your mind from your friends, and tempts you to go who knows where?

CHRISTIANA: I dreamt last night that I saw my dear Christian. Oh! that my soul were with him now! The Prince of the place has sent for me through one from on high, named Secret, who came to me at sun rise, and brought me this note to bid me go there. Do read it, I pray you.

TIMOROUS: Ah, you are mad to run such risks! You have heard, I am sure, from our friend Obstinate, what Christian met with on the way, for he and Pliable went with him; but they were wise and turned back home. You heard how he met with the beasts of prey and Apollyon, what he saw in the Valley of the Shadow of Death, and more still that makes my hair stand on end to hear of. I plead with you to think of these four sweet boys who are your own flesh and bone; and though you should be so rash as to wish to go yet for their sake, I pray you stay at home.

But Christiana said: "Do not tempt me. Now I have a chance to go forth and gain the truth, and I would be a fool if I had not the heart to grasp it. And these toils and snares that you tell me of shall not keep me back; no, they serve but to show me that what I do is right. Care must first be felt, then joy. So since you came not to my house in God's name, as I said, be gone from here, and tempt me no more."

Then Timorous said to Mercy (who had come with her), "Let us leave her in her own hands, since she scorns all that I say."

But Mercy thought that if her friend Christiana must leave, she would go part of the way with her to help her. She took some thought, too, of her own soul, for what Christiana had said had laid hold on her mind, and she felt she must talk with her friend; and if she found that truth and life were in her words, she would join her with all her heart.

Mercy cleaves to Christiana.

So Mercy said to Timorous: "I came with you to see Christiana, and since on this day she takes leave of the town, I think the least I can do would be to walk a short way with her, to help her on. But the rest of her heart she kept from Timorous.

TIMOROUS: Well, I see you have a mind to play the fool too; but take care in good time, and be wise.

So Mrs. Timorous went to her own house; and Christiana, with her four boys and Mercy, went on their way.

MERCY JOINS CHRISTIANA

Stage Two

y this time Christiana was on her way, and Mercy went with her; and so they went, with her sons by her side also.

"Mercy," said Christiana, "I take this as a great sign that you would help set me on my way."

Then said young Mercy (for she was quite young): "If I thought it would be good to join you, I would not go back at all to the town."

CHRISTIANA: Well, Mercy, cast your lot in with mine; I know what will be the great end of our toils. Christian is where he would not fail to be for all the gold in the mines of Spain. Nor shall you be sent back, if you look to Him; for the King who has sent for me and my boys is One who does not turn from those who seek Him. If you like, I will hire you, and you shall go as my maid, and you shall share all things with me.

MERCY: But how do I know that I shall be let in? If I thought I should have help from Him from whom all help comes, I would not wait, but would go at once, though the way be rough.

CHRISTIANA: Well, Mercy, I will tell you what I

would have you do. Go with me as far as to the field gate, and there I will ask; and if you see no hope there by Him who keeps the gate, you can go back to your home.

MERCY: Well, I will go with you, and the Lord grant that my lot may be cast to dwell in that land for which my heart yearns.

Christiana then felt glad that she had a friend to join her, and that this friend should have so great a care for her soul.

So they went on their way; but the face of Mercy was so sad that Christiana said to her: "What has caused you such pain? Why do you weep?"

MERCY: Oh, who could but weep to think of the state of my poor friends near and dear to me, in our bad town?

Mercy grieves for her friends in her town.

CHRISTIANA: You feel for your friends as my good Christian did for me when he left me, for it went to his heart to find that I would not see these things in the same light as he did. And now we, and these dear boys, reap the fruits of all his woes. I hope, Mercy, these tears of yours will not be shed in vain, for He who could not lie, has said that "they who sow in tears shall reap in joy." (Psalm 126:5)

Now when Christiana came up to the Slough of Despond, she and her sons made a stand, and Christiana told them that this was the place in which her dear Christian fell. But Mercy said: "Come, let us try; all we have to do is to keep the steps well in view.

Once or twice Christiana slipped in the mud; but at last they got through the Slough, and then they heard a voice say to them: "Blessed is she who has faith, for those things which were told her of the Lord shall come to pass."

So now they went on once more, and Mercy said: "If I had as much hope to get in at the gate as you have, I think no Slough of Despond would keep me back."

Mercy is bold at the Slough of Despond.

"Well," said Christiana, "it will be hard for both of us to reach the end; for how can we think that we who set out with thoughts and hopes of so much bliss, should steer clear of frights and fears on our way to that bright morn which it is our aim to reach?"

When they came to the gate, it took them some time to make out a plan of what they should say to him who stood there; and as Mercy was not as old as her friend, she said that it must rest with Christiana to speak for all of them.

So she gave a knock, and then (like Christian) two more; but no one came.

Now they heard the fierce bark of a dog, which made them shake with fear, so they did not dare for a while to knock a third time, lest the dog should fly at them. So they were put to their wits end to know what to do. To knock they did not dare, for fear of the dog; to go back they did not dare, or else He who kept the gate should see them as they went, and might not like it. At last they gave a knock four times as loud as the first.

Then He who stood at the gate said: "Who is there?" The dog was heard to bark no more, and the crate swung wide for them to come in.

Christiana sank on her knees, and said: "Let not our Lord be wroth that we have made such a loud noise at His gate."

At this He said: "From where do you come, and what is it that you want?"

CHRISTIANA: We are come from the town from where Christian came, to beg to be let in at this gate; that we may go on our way to The Celestial City. I was once the wife of Christian, who is now in the land of light and bliss.

With that, He who kept the gate threw up His arms and said: "What! Is she on her road to The Celestial City who, but a short time since, did hate the life of that place?"

Then Christiana bent her head, and said: "Yes, and so are these my dear sons." So He took her by the hand and led her in; and when her four sons had gone through, He shut the gate. This done, He said to a man who stood by: "Sound the horn for joy."

How Christiana came through the gate.

But now that Christiana was safe through the gate with her boys, she thought it time to speak a word for Mercy, so she said: "My Lord, I have a friend who stands at the gate, who has come here with the same trust that I did. One whose heart grieves to think that

THE KING'S TRUMPETER

she comes, when she is not sent for; while I had word from Christian's King to come."

The time did so lag with poor Mercy while she stood to be let in, that though it was but a short span, yet through fear and doubt did it seem to her like at least an hour; so Christiana could not say more for

MERCY COMES TO THE GATE

Mercy to Him who kept the gate. She knocked so fast, and so loud, that the noise made Christiana jump.

Then He said, "Who is there?"

CHRISTIANA: It is my friend.

So He threw back the gate to look out, but Mercy was faint from the fear that she should not be let in.

Then He took her by the hand, and said: "Fear not; stand firm on your feet, and tell me why you have come, and for what end?"

MERCY: I do not come as my friend Christiana does, for I was not sent for by the King, and I fear I am too bold. Yet if there is grace to share, I pray please let me share it.

Then He took her once more by the hand and led her in, and said: "All may come in who put their trust in me, let the means be what they may that brought them here."

Mercy is let in through the gate.

Then He told those that stood by to bring Mercy some myrrh, and in a while she got well.

And now Christiana and her boys and Mercy spoke to Him at the head of the way: "We are grieved at our sins, and beg of our Lord for His grace and peace."

"I grant it to thee," He said, "by my word and deed."

Then I saw in my dream that He spoke good words to Mercy, Christiana, and her boys, so as to make glad their hearts. And He took them up to the top of the gate, where He showed them by what deed they were saved; and told them of the sight they would have if they stayed firm on the way.

He left them for a while, and Christiana said: "Oh my dear friend, how glad am I that we have all got in!"

MERCY: It may be well with you; but I most of all have cause for joy.

CHRISTIANA: I thought at one time as I stood at the

gate, and no one came to me, that all our pains had been lost.

MERCY: But my worst fears came when I saw Him who kept the gate grant you your wish, and take no heed of me. And this brought to my mind the two who ground at the same mill, and how I was the one who was left; and I found it hard not to cry out, "I am lost! I am lost!"

CHRISTIANA: I thought you might have come in by brut force.

MERCY: Ah me! You saw that the door was shut on me, and that a fierce hound was not far off. Who, with so faint a heart as mine would not give loud knocks with all her might? But pray, what did my Lord say at this rude noise? Was He not wroth with me?

CHRISTIANA: When He heard your loud thumps at the door He gave a smile; and to my mind, what you did would seem to please Him well. But it is hard to guess why He keeps such a dog. Had I known of it, I fear I should not have wished to come in. But now we are in, we are safe; and I am glad with all my heart.

If the soul at first did know of all it should meet with on the way, it would never set out.

One of Christiana's boys said: "Please ask to have a chain put on the dog, or else it will bite us when we pass by."

Then He who kept the gate came down to them once more, and Mercy fell with her face to the ground, and said: "Oh, let me bless and praise the Lord with my lips!"

So He said to her: "Peace be to you; stand up."

But she would not rise till she had heard from Him why He kept so fierce a dog in the yard. He told her He did not own the dog, but that it was shut up in the grounds of one who dwelt near. "In truth," He said: "It is kept from no good will to me or mine, but to cause those who come here to turn back from my gate by the sound of its voice. But had you known more of me you would not have feared this dog. The poor man who goes from door to door will, for the sake of alms, run the risk of a bite; and shall a dog keep you from me?"

MERCY: I spoke of what I knew not; but Lord, I know that you do all things well.

Then Christiana rose as if she would go on her way. So He fed them, and set them in the right path, as He had done to Christian. And as they went, Christiana sang a hymn—"We turn our tears to joy, and our fears to faith."

"So Christiana's boys did pluck them and eat."

Stage Three

hey had not gone far when they saw some fruit trees, the boughs of which hung from the top of a wall that was built round the grounds of him who kept the fierce hound, and at times those that came that way would eat them to their cost. So as they were ripe, Christiana's boys threw them down and ate some of them; though Christiana did scold them for it, and said: "That fruit is not ours." But she did not know whose it was. Still the boys did eat of it.

The boys do eat of the foe's fruit.

Now when they had gone a bow shot from the place, they saw two men, who with bold looks came fast down the hill to meet them. With that, Christiana and her friend Mercy drew down their veils and so kept on their way.

Then the men came up to them, but Christiana said: "Stand back, or go by in peace, as you should." Yet they took no more heed of her words than if they had been deaf. Christiana, who did not like their looks, said: "We are in haste, and can not stay; our work is a work of life and death." With that, she and the rest made a fresh move to pass, but the men would not let them by.

"We intend no hurt to your lives." they answered.

"Ay," replied Christiana, "you would have us body and soul, for I know it is that for which you come."

So with one voice they all sent up a loud cry. Now, as they were not far from the field gate, they were heard from that place, and some of those in the lodge came out in haste to catch these bad men; when they soon leaped the wall, and got safe to the grounds where the dog was kept.

RELIEVER: How was it that when you were at the gate you did not ask Him who stood there to take you on your way, and guard you from harm? Had you done so you would not have gone through these frights, for He would have been sure to grant you your wish.

CHRISTIANA: Ah Sir, the joy we felt when we were let in, drove all fears from us; so who could have thought that so near the King's place there could have lurked such bad men? True, it would have been wise if we had thought to ask Him; but since our Lord knew it would be for our good, why did He not send someone with us?

RELIEVER: You did not ask. When the want of a thing is felt, that which we wish for is worth all the more.

CHRISTIANA: Shall we go back to my Lord and tell Him we wish we had been more wise, and ask for a guard?

RELIEVER: You need not go back, for in no place where you go will you find a want at all.

When he had said this he took his leave, and the rest went on their way.

MERCY: What a blank is here! I made sure we had been past all risk, and that we should see no more grief or pain.

CHRISTIANA: Your youth may plead for you, my friend, and shield you from blame; but as for me, my fault is so much worse, in so far as I knew what would take place when I had not yet come out of my door.

MERCY: But how could you know this when you had not yet set out?

CHRISTIANA: Why, I will tell you. One night as I lay in bed, I had a dream, in which I saw the whole scene as it took place just now.

By this time Christiana, Mercy, and the four boys had come to the house of Interpreter. Now when they drew near to the door they heard the sound of Christiana's name; for the news of her flight had made a great stir; but they did not know that she stood at the door. At

INNOCENT

last she gave a knock, as she had done at the gate, when there came to the door a young maid, whose name was Innocent.

INNOCENT: With whom would you speak in this place?

CHRISTIANA: As we heard that this is a place of rest for those that go by the way, we pray that we may be let in. As you can see, the day is far spent, and we yearn to rest for the night.

INNOCENT: Please tell me your name, that I may tell it to my Lord?

CHRISTIANA: My name is Christiana; I was the wife of Christian, who some time since came by this way, and these are his four sons.

Innocent then ran in, and said to those there: "Can you guess who is at the door? There are Christiana, her boys and her friend!"

There is joy in the house of the Interpreter.

So they leaped for joy, and went to tell it to their Lord, who came to the door and said: "Are you that Christiana whom Christian left in the town of Destruction, when he set out for The Celestial City?"

CHRISTIANA: I am she, and my heart was so hard as to slight his woes, and leave him to make his way on his own; and these are his four sons. But now I have come, for I feel sure that no way is right but this.

INTERPRETER: But why do you stand at the door? Come in! It was just now that we spoke of you, for we heard that you were on your way. Come, my dear boys, come in; come, my sweet maid, come in. So he took them to the house, and asked them to sit down and rest. All in the house wore a smile of joy to think that Christiana, was on her way to The Celestial City, and they were glad to see the young ones walk in God's ways, and shook their hand to show their good will. They said soft words, too, to Mercy, and made them all feel at ease. To fill up the time till they could eat, Interpreter took them to see all those things in the rooms that had been shown to Christian. When this was done, they were led to a room in which stood a man with a prong in his hand, who could look no way but down on the ground; and there stood one with a crown in his hand, which he said he would trade him for his prong; yet the first man did not look up, but went on to rake the straws, dust, and sticks which lay on the floor.

They see the man with the muck-rake.

Then said Christiana: "I think I know what this means. It is a sketch of a man of this world, is it not, good Sir?"

INTERPRETER: You are quite right, and his prong shows that his mind is of the earth, and that he thinks life in the next world is a mere song; take note that he does not so much as look up; and straws, sticks, and dust, with most are the great things to live for.

At that Christiana and Mercy wept, and said: "Ah, yes, it is too true!"

Interpreter then took them to a room where were a hen and her chicks, and made them look long at them. One of the chicks went to the trough to drink, and each time she drank she would lift up her head and

"A MAN THAT COULD LOOK NO WAY BUT DOWN, WITH A MUCK-RACK IN HIS HANDS."

her eyes to the sky.

"See what this bird does, and learn of her to know from where all good comes, and to give to the Lord who dwells on high, the praise and thanks for it. Look once more, and see all the ways that the hen has with her young brood. There is her call that goes on all day long; and there is her call that comes but now and then; she has a third call to shield them with her wings; and her fourth is a loud cry, which she gives when she spies a foe," spoke Interpreter.

"Now," he said, "set her ways by the side of your King's and the ways of these chicks by the side of those who love to do His will, and then you will see what I mean. For He has a way to walk in with His saints. By the call that comes all day He gives no heed; by a call that is rare He is sure to have some good to give; then there is a call, too, for those that would come to His wings, which He spreads out to shield them; and He has a cry to warn men from those who might hurt their souls. I choose scenes from real life, as they are not too hard for you to grasp, when I fit them to your own case; and it is the love I have for your souls that prompts me to show you these things."

CHRISTIANA: Pray, let us see some more.

Interpreter then took them to his field, which was sown with wheat and corn; but when they came to look, the ears were cut off, and there was none but the straw left.

INTERPRETER: What shall we do with this crop?

CHRISTIANA: Burn some, and use the rest to dress the ground with.

INTERPRETER: Fruit, you see, is the thing you look for, and for want of that you cast off the whole crop. Take heed that in this you do not seal your own doom: for by fruit I mean works.

Now when they came back to the house the meal was not yet spread, so Christiana begged of Interpreter to show or tell them some more things.

INTERPRETER: So much the more strong a man's health is, so much the more prone is he to sin. The more fat the cow is, the more she loves the mire. It is not so hard to sit up a night or two, as to watch for a whole year; just as it is not so hard to start well as it is to hold out to the end. One leak will sink a ship, and one sin will kill a man's soul. If a man would live well, let him keep his eyes on his last day.

The table was then spread and they did eat of all things set on the board.

Now when Christiana, Mercy, and the boys had a good night's rest, they rose with the sun, and made a move to leave; but the Interpreter would have them stay a while. "For," he said, "you must go at the right time, such is the rule of the house."

They take the bath of Sanctification

Then he told Innocent to take them to the bath, and there wash the dust from them. This done, they came forth fresh and strong, and as Interpreter said: "Fair as the moon."

Next he told those near him to bring the seal, and

when it was brought he set his mark on them, that they might be known in each place where they went.

Then said Interpreter: "Bring vests for them." And they were dressed in robes as white as snow, so that it made each start to see the rest shine with so bright a light.

He seeks to flee the wrath to come.

Interpreter then sent for one of his men whose name was Great-heart, and gave the word that he should be dressed in a coat of mail, with sword and shield, and that he should take them to the house Beautiful, where they would rest.

Then Interpreter took his leave of them, with a good wish for each. So they went on their way, and thus they sang:

"0 move me, Lord, to watch and pray,
From sin my heart to clear;
To take my cross up day by day,
And serve the Lord with fear."

MR. GREAT-HEART

Stage Four

ow I saw in my dream that these all went on, with Great-heart by their side. They next came to the place where Christian's load fell off his back and was lost in the tomb. Here they paused, and blessed God. "Now," said Christiana, "it comes to mind what was said to us at the gate—that we should be set free by word and deed. Mr. Great-heart, if you please, might you tell us what this means?

MR. GREAT-HEART: Pardon by the work done is by one that has no need of it. It was by Him that let you in at the gate. He has spilt His own blood to wash you from your sin.

How the strings of the load of sin were cut.

CHRISTIANA: But if He parts with His good for us, what has He left for His own?

MR. GREAT-HEART: He has more than you need of. Also, I must tell you that He is more than you saw; He is two in one—both man and God. It is by His work that you may be deemed right in the eyes of God; and it was by this truth that those strings which held Christian's load, were cut from off his back.

CHRISTIANA: This is brave! Now I see what is to be

learned by word and deed as the means to be freed from sin.

Now I saw in my dream that they went up till they had come to the place where Simple, Sloth, and Presumption lay and slept when Christian went on his way; and I saw they were hanged up in chains a ways off on one side.

Great-heart tells of the three bad men.

Then Mercy said to Great-heart, their guide: "What are these three men, and for what are they hanged?"

GREAT-HEART: These three men were bad in all things; they had no mind to go on the path which leads to life, and they sought whom they could to go as well on their way of doom.

MERCY: But could they turn any to go with them?

GREAT-HEART: Yes, some went out of the way. There was Slow-pace, and one Short-wind with No-heart, Linger-after and Sleepy-head, as well as a young girl named Dull, who went with them.

MERCY: Well, let them now hang and their names rot, and their crimes live on that none may fall as their prey.

Thus they went on till they came to the hill Difficulty, which they went up. It was so steep that the work made Christiana pant for breath.

"How can we doubt," she said, "that they who love rest more than their souls would choose some way on which they could go with more ease than this?"

Then Mercy said: "Come what may, I must rest here

for a while."

And James, who was the least of the boys, cried for rest.

"Come, come!" said Great-heart, "do not sit down here; for there is a seat near us put there by the Prince. With this he took the young child by the hand, and led him to it; and they were all glad to sit down, and to be out of the heat of the sun's rays."

Then said Mercy: "How sweet is rest to them that work! And how good is the Prince to place this seat here that such as we may rest! I have heard much of this spot, but let us take care that we do not sleep, for that cost poor Christian much."

Then, said Mr. Great-heart: "Well, my brave boys, how do you do? What do you think of this hill?"

"Sir," said James, "this hill beats me out of heart! And I see now that what I have been told is true, the land of bliss is up steps; but still, Sir, it is worse to go down hill to death than up hill to life."

"You are a good boy," said Great-heart.

At this, Mercy could but smile, and it made James

blush.

CHRISTIANA: Come, will you not drink out of this flask, and eat some fruit, while we sit here to rest? For Mr. Interpreter put these in my hand as I came out of his door.

MERCY: I thought I saw him place some thing in your hands.

CHRISTIANA: So he did, and it shall be as I spoke when we first came from home; you shall share in all the good that I have, for you so did choose to come with me.

Then she gave to them and they did eat, both Mercy and the boys.

GIANT GRIM

Stage Five

ow when they had sat there a while, their guide said to them: "The day runs on, and if you think well of it, let us now go on our way."

So they all set out, the boys first, then the rest; but they had not gone far when Christiana found she had left the flask, so she sent James back to fetch it.

Christiana loses her flask.

MERCY: I think this is the place where Christian lost his scroll. How was this, Sir?

GREAT-HEART: We may trace it to two things; one is sleep, and one is that you cease to think of that which you cease to want: and when you lose sight of a boon† you lose sight of Him who grants it, and the joy of it will end in tears.

By and by they came to a small mound with a post on it, where these words were cut, "Let him who sees this post take heed that he lie not in his heart or with his tongue." Then they went on till they came up to two large beasts of prey.

Now Great-heart was a strong man, so he had no fear; but their fierce looks made the boys scared, and

---

† A blessing

they all clung round Great-heart.

"How is this, my boys! You march on first, as brave as can be, when there is no cause for fear; but when a test of your strength comes you shrink."

Now when Great-heart drew his sword to force a way there came up one Giant Grim, who said, in a gruff voice: "What right have you to come here?"

GREAT-HEART: These folk are on their way to The Celestial City, and this is the road they shall go, in spite of you and the wild beasts.

GIANT GRIM: This is not their way, nor shall they go on it. I have come forth to stop them, and to that end will back the wild beasts.

Now, to speak truth, so fierce were these beasts, and so grim the looks of him who had charge of them, that the road was grown with weeds and grass from want of use. And still Grim warned them to turn; "you shall not pass," he said.

The fight twixt Giant Grim and Great-heart.

But their guide came up, and struck so hard at him with his sword as to force him to fall back.

GIANT GRIM: Will you slay me on my own ground?

GREAT-HEART: It is the King's high way on which we stand, and in His way it is that you have put these beasts. But these, who are in my charge, though weak, shall hold on in spite of all.

And with that he dealt him a blow that brought him to the ground; and so Giant Grim was slain.

Then Great-heart said: "Come now with me, and you shall see no harm from the two beasts." So they went by, but shook from head to foot at the mere sight of the beast's teeth and claws.

At length they came in sight of the lodge, to which they soon went up, but rushed to get there as it grew dark. So when they had come to the gate the guide knocked, and the man at the lodge said in a loud voice: "Who goes there?"

GREAT-HEART: It is I, Mr. Great-heart.

MR. WATCHFUL: How now, Mr. Great-heart? What has brought you here at so late an hour?

Then Great-heart told him that he had come with some friends on their way to Zion.

MR. WATCHFUL: Will you go in and stay till the day dawns?

GREAT-HEART: No, I will go back to my Lord this night.

CHRISTIANA: O, Sir, we can not part with you now, for it is to your stout heart that we owe our lives. You have fought for us, you have taught us what is right, and your faith and your love have known no bounds.

MERCY: O, that we could have you for our guide all the rest of the way! For how can such weak folk as we hold out in a path fraught with toils and snares if we have no friend like you to take us?

JAMES: Pray, Sir, stay with us and help us. The way we go is so hard to find.

GREAT-HEART: As my Lord wills, so must I do. If He sends me to join you once more, I shall be glad to wait on you. But it was here that you were in fault at first, for when He called me to come this far with you, if you had said, "We beg of you to let him go all the way with us," He would have let me do so. But now I must go back; and so good Christiana, Mercy, and my dear boys, fare ye all well.

Great-heart must leave them.

Then did Watchful, who kept the lodge, ask Christiana where she had come from, and who her friends were.

CHRISTIANA: I come from the City of Destruction, and I was the wife of Christian, who is now in bliss.

Then Watchful rang the bell, and there came to the door a maid, to whom he said: "Go, make it known that Christiana, the wife of Christian, and her four boys have come, on their way to The Celestial City."

So she went in and told all this. And, oh, what shouts of joy were sent forth when those words fell from her mouth? So all rushed up to Watchful; for Christiana still stood at the door.

Then some of the most grave spoke to her: "Christiana, come in, wife of that good man; come in, blessed one; come in, with all that are with you."

So she went in, and the rest with her. Then they all sat down in a large room, where the chief of the house came to see them and to cheer up his guests. Then he gave each of them a kiss. But since it was quite late, and Christiana and the rest were faint from the great trial they had come through, they sought to rest.

"Nay", said those of the house, "take first some meat;" for as Watchful had heard that they were on their way, a lamb had been slain for them. When the meal had come to an end, and they had sung a psalm, Christiana said: "If we may be so bold as to choose, let us rest in that room which was Christian's when he was here."

So they took them there, but as she went to sleep Christiana said: "I did not think when my poor Christian set off with his load on his back that I should do the same."

MERCY: No, nor did you think then that you should rest in the same room as he had done.

CHRISTIANA: And less still to see his dear face once more, and to praise the Lord the King with him; and yet now I think I shall!

MERCY: Do you hear a noise?

CHRISTIANA: Yea! As far as I can make out, the sounds we now hear come from the lute, the pipe, and the horn.

MERCY: Sweet sounds in the house, sweet sounds in the air, sweet sounds in the heart, for joy that we are here!

Thus did Christiana and Mercy talk a while, and then they slept.

Now at dawn when they woke up, Christiana said to Mercy, "What was it that made you laugh in your sleep last night? Were you in a dream?"

MERCY: Yes, and a sweet dream it was. But are you sure that I did laugh?

CHRISTIANA: Yes, you laughed as if from your heart of hearts. Do pray Mercy tell it to me.

MERCY: I dreamt that I lay, in some lone wood to weep and wail, for that my heart should be so hard. Now I had not been there long when I thought there were some who had come to hear me speak in my sleep; but I went on with my moans. At this they said with a laugh, that I was a fool. Then I saw a Bright One with wings come up to me, who said: "Mercy, why do you weep?" And when he heard the cause of my grief, he said: "Peace be to you." He then came up to wipe off my tears, and had me dressed in robes of gold, and put a chain on my neck, and a crown on my head. Then he took me by the hand and said: "Mercy, come this way." So he went up with me till we came to a gate, at which he knocked, and then he took me to a throne on which the great One sat. The place was as bright as the stars;—no, more like the sun. And I thought I saw Christian

Mercy's dream.

there. So I woke from my dream. But did I laugh?

CHRISTIANA: Laugh! Yes, and so you might, to see how well off you were! For you must let me tell you, that as you find the first part true, so you will find the last.

MERCY: Well, I am glad of my dream, for I hope I do not have to wait long to see it come to pass, so as to make me laugh once more.

CHRISTIANA: I think it is now time for us to be on our way.

MERCY: Please, if they should ask us to stay, let us

PRUDENCE TAUGHT THE BOYS OF THE THINGS OF GOD.

by all means do so; for I would like to know more of these maids. I do think Prudence, Piety, and Charity are most kind.

CHRISTIANA: We shall see what they will do.

So they came down.

Then said Prudence and Piety: "If you will stay here, you shall have what the house will give."

CHARITY: Yes, and that with good will.

So they were there some time, much to their good.

PRUDENCE: Christiana, I give you all praise, for you have brought your boys up well. With James I have had a long chat; he is a good boy, and has learned much that will bring peace to his mind while he lives on this earth, and in the world to come it will cause him to see the face of Him who sits on the throne. For my own part, I will teach all your sons.

"At the same time," said she to the boys, "you must still give heed to all that Christiana will teach you; but more than that, you must read the Book of God's Word, which sent your dear dad on his way to the land of joy and bliss.

By the time that Christiana and the rest had been there a week, a man, Mr. Brisk by name, came to woo Mercy, and wished to wed her. Now Mercy was fair to look on, and her mind was at all times set on work and the care of those round her. She would knit for the poor, and give to all those things of which they stood in need.

Mr. Brisk woos Mercy to wed him.

"She will make me a good housewife," thought Mr.

Brisk.

Mercy one day said to those of the house: "Will you tell me what you think of Mr. Brisk?"

They then told her that the young man would seem to have a great sense of the love of God, but that they had fears it did not reach his soul, which they thought did cleave too much to this world.

"Well then," said Mercy, "I will look no more on him, for I will not have a clog to my soul."

PRUDENCE: If you go on as you have set out, and work hard for the poor, he will soon leave.

So the next time he came, he found her at her work.

"What! Still at it?" he said.

MERCY: Yes.

MR. BRISK: How much can you earn in the day?

MERCY: I work at these things for the good of those for whom I do them; and more than this, to do the will of Him who was slain on the cross for me.

With that his face fell, and he came to see her no more.

PRUDENCE: Did I not tell you that Mr. Brisk would soon flee from you? Yea, he may seem to love Mercy, but Mercy and he could not tread the same road of life side by side.

Now Matthew, the son of Christiana, fell sick, so they sent to Mr. Skill to cure him. Then he said, "Tell me, what did he eat?"

Matthew falls sick from the fruit he ate.

CHRISTIANA: Well, there is no food here but what is good.

Mr. Skill

MR. SKILL: This boy has in him a crude mass of food, which if I do not use the means to get rid of, he will die.

Samuel said to Christiana, "What was it that you saw Matthew pick up and eat when we came from the gate which is at the head of this way?"

CHRISTIANA: It was some of the fruit that grows there; which I told him not to touch.

SKILL: I felt sure that it was some bad food; now that fruit hurts more than all, for it is the fruit from Beelzebub's grounds. Did no one warn you of it? Some fall down dead when they eat it.

Then Christiana wept and said: "What shall I do for my son? Please, Sir, try your best to cure him, let it cost what it may."

Then Skill gave strange drugs to him, which he would not take. So Christiana put one of them to the tip of her tongue. "Oh Matthew," she said, "it is sweet, sweet as balm; if you love me, if you love Mercy, if you love your life, do take it."

So in time he did, and felt grief for his sin. He soon lost the pain, so that with a staff he could walk, and went from room to room to talk with Mercy, Prudence, Piety, and Charity. They brought to him great words of cheer and joy from God's Word.

Matthew comes to know grief over his sin.

CHRISTIANA: Pray, Sir, tell me what else are these pills good for?

SKILL: They are good for all those that go on their

way to the Celestial City.

CHRISTIANA: I plead with you to make me up a large box full of them, for if I can get these, I will take none else.

SKILL: There is no doubt that if a man will use them as he should, he would not die. But, good Christiana, these pills will be of no use if you do not give them as I have done,—that is, in a glass of grief for the sins of those who take them.

So he gave some to Christiana and the rest of her boys, and to Mercy. He urged Matthew to keep a good look out that he ate no more green apples. Then he gave him a kiss, and went his way.

Now, as they had spent some time here, they made a move to go. Then Joseph, who was Christiana's third son, said to her: "You were to send word to the house of Mr. Interpreter to beg of him to grant that Mr. Great-heart should go with us as our guide."

"Good, my son!" said Christiana, "I had not thought of it."

So she wrote a note, and Interpreter said to the man who brought it: "Go, tell them that I will send him."

Great-heart soon came, and he said to Christiana and Mercy: "My Lord has sent you some wine and parched corn, and to the boys figs and dry grapes, to give you strength for the way."

They then set off, and Prudence and Piety went with them. When they came to the gate, Christiana asked Watchful: "Have you seen men go by since we have been here?"

WATCHFUL: Yes, I have, and there has been a great theft on this high way; but the thieves were caught.

Then Christiana and Mercy said they felt great fear to go on that road.

MATTHEW: Fear not, as long as we have Mr. Great-heart with us as our guide.

Great-heart comes back to be their guide.

Then Christiana said: "Dear Watchful, I give you thanks for your kind acts shown to me since I've been here, and also your love shown to my kin." She put a small coin in his hand while she gave him her thanks. So he bowed down to her and said: "Let your robes always be white, and let your head want of no oil. Let Mercy live and not die, and let not her works be few." And to the boys he spoke: "Do flee the lusts of youth, and go with those that are grave and wise; so shall the heart of your dear Christiana might be glad and the praise from those that love God will be on you."

So they all thanked Watchful and went on their way.

Stage Six

 now saw in my dream that they went on till they came to the brow of the hill, when Piety said: "Oh, I must go back to fetch that which I meant to give to Christiana and Mercy. It was a list of all those fine things which they had seen at our house. I beg of you to look on them from time to time, and call them to mind for your good."

They now went down the hill to the Valley of Humiliation. It was a steep hill, and their feet slid as they went on; but they took great care, and when they came to the foot of it, Piety said to Christiana: "This is the vale where Christian met with Apollyon, and where they had that fierce fight which I know you must have heard of. But be of good cheer, as long as we have Mr. Great-heart to guide us, there is not a thing here that will hurt us, save those sights that spring from our own fears. When the good folk of the town hear that such a bad thing fell out in such a place, to the hurt of such a one, think that some foul fiend haunts that place, when it is from the fruit of their own ill deeds that such things

They come to the Valley of Humiliation.

AS THE BOY SAT ON A BANK, HE SANG A SONG

fall on them. For they that make slips must look for frights. And this is why the vale has so bad a name.

JAMES: See, there is a post with words on it, I will go and read them.

So he went, and found that these words were cut on it: "Let the slips which Christian met with when he came here, and the fights he had in this place, warn all those who come to the Valley of Humiliation."

MR. GREAT-HEART: It is not so hard to go up as down this hill, and that can be said of but few hills in this part of the world. But we will leave the good man; he is at rest, and he had a brave fight with the foe. Let Him who dwells on high grant that we fare no worse when our strength comes to be put to the test. This vale brings forth much fruit. *The Valley is a brave place where men thrive.*

Now, as they went on, they met a boy who was dressed in poor clothes and kept watch on some sheep. He had a fine fresh face, and as he sat on a bank he sang a song.

"Hark", said Great-heart, "to the words of that boy's song."

So they gave ear to it:

"He that is down need fear no fall,
He that is low, no pride,
He that is meek at all times shall
Have God to be his guide."

Then said Great-heart: "Do you hear him? I dare say this boy is as full of cheer as he that is dressed in silk, and that he wears more of that plant which they call heart's ease."

SAMUEL: Ask Great-heart in what part of this vale it was that Apollyon came to fight Christian?

GREAT-HEART: The fight took place at that part of the plain which has the name of Forgetful Green. And if those who go on their way meet with a shock, it is when they lose sight of the good which they have at the hand of Him who dwells on high.

MERCY: I think I feel as well in this place as I have done in all the rest of our way. This vale has a sweet air, that just suits my mind; for I love to be in such a spot as this, where there are no coach wheels to make a noise. Here one may think a while what he is, from where he came, and for what the King has made him. Here one may think and pray.

Just then they thought that the ground they trod on shook. But the guide urged them to be of good cheer, and look well to their feet, lest by chance they should meet with some snare.

Then James felt sick, but I think the cause of it was fear, and Christiana gave him some of the wine which Mr. Interpreter had put in her hands, and three of the pills, which Mr. Skill had made up, and the boy was soon well.

They then went on a while, and Christiana said: "What is that thing on the road? A thing of such a shape I have not seen in all my life!"

Joseph said: "What is it?"

"A vile thing, child; a vile thing!" she said.

JOSEPH: But what is it like?

CHRISTIANA: It is like, I can't tell what. Just then it was far off, now it is close.

GREAT-HEART: Well, well, let them that fear the most keep close to me.

The fiend comes to strike fear in them all.

Then it went out of sight of all of them.

But they had not gone far when Mercy looked back, and saw a great beast rush upon them with a loud roar.

This noise made them all quake with fright, all but their guide, who fell back and put the rest in front of him. But when the brute saw that Great-heart meant to fight him, he drew back and was seen no more.

Now they had not left the spot long when a great mist fell on them, so that they could not see.

"What shall we do?" they said.

Their guide told them not to fear, but to stand still, and see what an end he would put to this.

Then Christiana said to Mercy: "Now I see what my poor dear Christian went through. I have heard much of this place. Poor man, he went here in the dead of the night, and no one with him; but who can tell what the Valley of the Shadow of Death should mean, till they come to see it? To be here fills my breast with awe!"

The Valley of the Shadow of Death.

GREAT-HEART: It seems now as if the earth and its bars were round us. I would not boast, but I trust we shall still make our way. Come, let us pray for light to Him that can give it.

So did they weep and pray. And as the path was now more smooth, they went straight on.

MERCY: To be here is not as sweet as it was at The Gate, or at Mr. Interpreter's, or at the house where we were last.

"Oh," said one of the boys, "it is not so bad to go through this place as it is to dwell here for all time; for I am sure we have to go this way that our home may seem to us more sweet."

GREAT-HEART: Well said, Samuel; now you speak like a man.

SAMUEL: Why, if I get out of this place, I think I shall prize that which is light and good more than I have done in all my life.

GREAT-HEART: We shall be out soon.

So on they went.

JOSEPH: Can we not see to the end of this vale yet?

GREAT-HEART: Look to your feet, for you will soon be where the snares are.

So they took heed.

GREAT-HEART: Men come here and bring no guide with them, and so they die from

HEEDLESS SLAIN!

the snares they meet within the way.

Now when they came to the snares, they spied a man in a ditch on the left hand, with his flesh all torn.

GREAT-HEART: That is one named Heedless, who was slain on the way and has lain here a great while.

"Poor Christian!" thought Christiana. "It is strange he should have got out of this place, and been safe. But God dwelt in his soul, and he had a stout heart of his own, or else he could not have done it."

FATHER HONEST

Stage Seven

ow I saw that as they went on the way, there stood an oak tree; where they found an old friend, Father Honest, fast to sleep. So the guide, Mr. Great-heart, woke him, and he cried out, "Who are you? Come, my dear man, here are none but friends. My name is Great-heart, I am the guide for these that are on their way to the Celestial City."

HONEST: I feared that you were with those who robbed Little-Faith, but as I look at you I see you are those I can trust.

GREAT-HEART: Well, now that we have met, please tell me your name and the place you came from.

HONEST: My name is Old Honest, and I have come from a town called Stupidity, past the City of Destruction. It is a very cold place, yet if the Sun of Righteousness would shine on a man's hard heart, it shall melt; just as it has done with me.

Then the old man bowed to them all, asked them their names, and they spoke more of how they fared since they set out on their way.

Now as they walked on, the guide asked the old

MR. FEARING IN THE SLOUGH OF DESPOND

man if he knew one, named Mr. Fearing, who came
out from his town as well.

HONEST: Knew him! I was a friend to him, and was
with him a long time. He knew many things of our
Lord, yet he had no peace in his soul, and thought too
much of what could come of us as we went on the
way.

GREAT-HEART: I know full well that it is as you say,
for I was his guide from my Master's house to the
gates of the Celestial City. For in my trip with him, I
was called to bear with him, with cheer, just as he was.

HONEST: Then, I pray, tell how it was with him.

GREAT-HEART: Well, everything he heard or saw
caused him much fear, and he fell at every straw that

was cast in his way. He even lay at the Slough of Despond for more than a month. One day, I don't know how, he got out of it; yet he had a Slough of Despond in his mind, a slough that went with him whereever he went, or else he could not have been as sad as he was. As we went on the way, we came to Interpreter's door, where he had seen many great things, and Interpreter gave him some good things to eat, but Fearing was of few words, and many sighs.

It would be too much to tell you all, so I will speak of a few more. When he came to Vanity Fair, I thought he would have fought with all the men at the fair. I feared there we would be both knocked on the head, for so hot was he at them. At the Enchanted Ground he felt quite pleased, but when he reached the River of Death where there was no bridge, he was then in a sad state. But the River was low at that time, so he went through it at last. And so I took my leave of him with much joy and peace.

It is well with Mr. Fearing.

HONEST: Then it was well with him at last?

GREAT-HEART: I have no doubt.

Now I saw in my dream that they went on in their talk. For after Great-heart had made an end with Mr. Fearing, Mr. Honest told them of one named Mr. Self-will. "He wished to be a true one on the way," said Mr. Honest, "yet I knew he did not come in at the gate."

GREAT-HEART: Did you speak to him of it?

HONEST: Yes, more than once or twice, but he was

self-willed at all times. He did not care for man at all, but what his mind would say, that he would do.

CHRISTIANA: I wish that there was an inn here where we could all rest.

"Well," said Mr. Honest, "there is such a place not far off."

So there they went, and the host, whose name was Gaius said: "Come in, for my house was built for such as you."

GREAT-HEART: Good Gaius, let us dine. What have you for us to eat? We have gone through great pains,

and stand much in want of food.

They taste that which is good, from Gaius.   GAIUS: It is too late for us to go out and find food; but what we have you shall eat.

The meal was then spread, and near the end of the feast all sat round the board to crack nuts, when old Honest said to Gaius: "Please, sir, tell me what this verse means?"

"There was a man, and some did count him mad;
The more that this man gave the more he had."

Then all the youths gave a guess as to what Gaius would say to it; so he sat still a while, and then said:

"He that gives his goods to the poor,
shall have as much and ten times more."

JOSEPH: I did not think, Sir, that you would have found it out.

GAIUS: Ah! I have learned of my Lord to be kind, and I find I gain much by it.

Then Samuel said in a low voice to Christiana: "This is a good man's house; let us stay here awhile, and why should Matthew not wed Mercy here?"

Gaius heard him say this and said: "With all my heart." And he gave Mercy to Matthew as his wife.

By this time Christiana's son, James, had come of age, and Gaius gave Phebe (who was his child) to be his wife. They spent ten more days at the house of Gaius, and then took their leave. But on the last day he made them a feast, of

GAIUS BRINGS GOOD FOOD

which they all ate and drank.

GAIUS: Now, since you are all here, let us walk through the fields, to see if we can do any good. Up a mile there is one named Giant Slay-good, that does much to harm the King's high way in these parts; and I know where his cave is. He leads a mass of thieves, so it would be well if we could rid these parts of him.

So they went on, Mr. Great-heart with his sword and shield, and the rest with spears and staves.

When they came to the place where he was, they found him with a poor soul named Feeble-mind in his hand, whom his slaves had brought to him from the way. Well, so soon as he saw Mr. Great-heart and his friends at the mouth of his cave, with their arms, he sought to know why they had come.

Giant Slay-good and Feeble-mind.

GREAT-HEART: We want you! For we have come in the name of those that you have dragged out of the King's high way and slain. Come out of your cave!

So he came out and they fought for more than an hour. The fight was fierce, but Mr. Great-heart was stout, so he struck him, and slew him, and cut off his head. They then went back to the inn, with Feeble-mind safe by their side.

GREAT-HEART: Now, Gaius, the hour has come that we must be gone; so tell me what I owe you for this long stay at your inn, for we have been here for many days.

GAIUS: At my house no one pays; for the good

GIANT SLAY-GOOD IN HIS CAVE

Samaritan told me that I was to look to him for all the charge that I was owed.

They now took leave of him and they met with all kinds of frights and fears, till they came to a place which bore the name of Vanity Fair. There they went to the house of Mr. Mnason, who said to his guests: "If there be a thing that you stand in need of, say so, and we will do what we can to get it for you."

They reach Vanity Fair and Mr. Mnason.

"Well, then," said they, "we would like to see some of the good folk in this town."

So Mnason stamped his foot on the ground, at which time Grace came up, and he sent her to fetch some of his friends who were in the house, and they

all sat down to a meal.

Then said Mr. Mnason, as he held out his hand to point to Christiana: "My friends, I have guests here who are on their way to Zion. But who do you think this is? This is the wife of Christian, whom (with his friend Faithful) the men of this town did treat so ill."

"Well," said they, "who would have thought to meet Christiana at this place! May the King whom you love and serve bring you to where Christian is, in peace!"

They then told her that the blood of Faithful had lain like a load on their hearts; and that since they had burned him no more men had been sent to the stake at Vanity Fair. "In those days," said they, "good men could not walk the streets, but now they can show their heads."

Christiana and her sons and Mercy made this place their home for some years, and in the course of time Mr. Mnason, who had a wife and two girls, gave his first born, whose name was Grace, to Samuel as his wife, and Martha to Joseph.

Now, one day, a huge snake came out of the woods and slew some of the folk of the town. None of these were so bold as to dare to face him, but all fled when they heard that he came near, for he took off with babes by scores.

But Great-heart and the rest of the men who were at Mr. Mnason's house, made up their minds to kill this snake, and so rid the town of him. So they went forth to meet him, and at first the snake did not seem to heed them; but as they were strong men at arms, they drove him back. Then they lay in wait for him, and fell on him, till at last he died of his wounds. By this deed Mr. Great-heart and the rest won the good will of the whole town.

DOUBTING CASTLE IS TORN DOWN

Stage Eight

he time drew near for them to go on their way. Mr. Great-heart went first as their guide; and I saw in my dream that they came to the stream on this side of The Delectable Mountains, where fine trees grew on each bank, the leaves of which were good for the health, and the fields were green all the year round; and here they might lie down and be safe. Here, too, there were folds for sheep, and a house was built in which to rear the lambs, and there was One who kept watch on them, who would take them in His arms and lay them in His breast.

The stream by the Delectable Mountains.

Now Christiana urged the four young wives to place their babes by the side of this stream, so that they might not lack in time to come: "For," she said, "if they should stray or be lost, He will bring them back; He will give strength to the sick, and here they shall not want meat, drink, or clothes." So they left their young ones in His care.

When they went to ByPath Meadow they sat on the fence to which Christian had gone with Hopeful, when Giant Despair shut the two up in Doubting

Castle. They sat down to think if it would be right to pull down Doubting Castle, now that they were so strong a force, and had such a man as Mr. Great-heart to guide them; and should there be poor souls shut up there who were on their way to The Celestial City, they would be set free. One said this thing, and one said that; at last Mr. Great-heart said: "We are told in the book of God's Word, that we are to fight the good fight. And, I pray, with whom should we fight if not with Giant Despair? So who will go with me?"

The fight with Giant Despair and Diffidence.

Christiana's four sons said: "We will;" for they were young and strong; so they left their wives and went.

When they knocked at the gate, Giant Despair and his wife, Diffidence, came out to them.

GIANT DESPAIR: Who and what is he that is so bold as to come to the gate of Giant Despair?

GREAT-HEART: It is I, Great-heart, a guide to those who are on their way to Zion. And I charge you to throw wide your gates and stand forth, for I have come to slay you and pull down your house.

GIANT DESPAIR: What, shall such as Great-heart make me fear? No, I think not.

So he put a cap of steel on his head, and with a breast plate of fire, and a club in his hand, the giant came out to fight his foes.

Then these six men came up to him, and they fought for their lives, till Despair was brought to the ground, and put to death by Great-heart. Next they

THE MONUMENT OF DELIVERANCE FROM THE GRIP OF GIANT DESPAIR

fell on his house, but it took six days to pull it down. They found there Mr. Despondency and one Muchafraid, his child, and set them free.

Then they all went on to The Delectable Mountains. They made friends with the men that kept watch on their flocks, who were as kind to them as they had been to Christian and Hopeful.

"You have brought a good group with you," they said. "Pray, where did you find them?"

So their guide told them how it had come to pass. Then they showed them places both good and bad. One such place was Mount Innocence. There they saw a man clothed in all white, and two men, Prejudice and Ill-will, that cast dirt on him. Now, the dirt they cast on him, would, in a short time, fall off; and the robe he wore would look as clean as if no dirt had been thrown.

GREAT-HEART: What does this mean?

ILL-WILL

SHEPHERDS: This man is named Godly-man, and the robe he wears is to show how pure his life is. Now those that throw dirt at him are those who hate his good deeds; but as you can see, the dirt will not stick to his clothes. So shall it be with him that lives right in the world. And those who would seek to make men full of dirt, their work is in vain; for God will see to it that they who do right shall break forth as the light and their deeds as the noon day.

VALIANT-FOR-TRUTH

Stage Nine

y and by they went on, and just at the place where Little-faith had been robbed, there stood a man with his sword drawn, and his face all over with blood.

GREAT-HEART: Who are you?

The man said, "I am one whose name is Valiant-for-truth. I am on my way to the Celestial City. Now as I went forth, three men, Wild-head, Inconsiderate, and Pragmatic, sought to stop me in the path. As they drew towards me, I drew to them, and we fell to it. For more than three hours, I fought as though my sword and my hand were one, till I felt blood run through my hands."

Valiant-for-truth battles the forces of sin.

GREAT-HEART: You have done well, for you have won the fight with sin. Come with us, for we seek the same prize as you.

By and by they came to The Enchanted Ground, where the air makes men sleep. Now they had not gone far, when a thick mist fell on them, so that for a while they could not see; and as they could not walk by sight, they kept near their guide by the help of words. But one fell in a bush, while one stuck fast in

THE ENCHANTED GROUND

the mud, and some of the young ones lost their shoes in the mire. "Oh, I am down!" said one. "Where are you?" cried the next. While a third said: "I am stuck in this bush."

Then they came to a bench, (Slothful's Friend by name) which had shrubs and plants round it, to screen those who sat there from the sun. But Christiana and the rest warned them of what their guide told them, that though they were worn out with toil, yet there was not one of them that had so much as a wish to stop there; for they knew that it would be death to sleep for a short time on The Enchanted Ground.

Now since it was still dark, their guide struck a light that he might look at his map (the book of God's Word), and had he not done so, they would all have been lost, for just at the end of the road was a pit, full of mud, which no one can tell how deep.

Then I thought: "Who is there who would have one of these maps or books in which he may look when he is in doubt, and knows not which way to take?"

They soon came to a bench, on which sat two men, Heedless and Too-bold; and Christiana and the rest shook their heads, for they saw that these men were in a bad case. They knew not what they ought to do—to go on and leave them in their sleep, or to try to wake them. Now the guide who knew them both, spoke to them by name; but he did not hear a sound from their lips. So Great-heart at last shook them, and did all he could to wake them.

One of the two, whose name was Heedless, said: "Let me be! I will pay you when I bring in my debts."

At this the guide shook his head.

Then Too-bold spoke: "Out! I will fight as long as I can hold my sword."

When he had said this, all who stood round laughed at him.

CHRISTIANA: What does that mean ?

GREAT-HEART: They talk in their sleep. If you strike or shake them, they will still talk in the same way, for their sleep is like that of the man on the mast of a ship, when the waves of the sea, beat on him.

Then did Christiana, Mercy, and their group go on with fear, and they sought from their guide a light for the rest of the Way.

But as the poor babes' cries were loud for want of rest, all fell on their knees to pray for help. And by the time they had gone a short way, a wind sprang up which drove off the fog. So, now that the air was clear, they made their way.

Then they came to the land of Beulah, where the sun shines night and day. Here they took some rest, and ate of the fruit that hung from the boughs round them. But all the sleep that they could wish for in such a land as this was but for a short time; for the bells rang to such sweet tunes, and such a blaze of lights burst on their eyes, that they soon rose to walk to and fro on this bright way, where no base feet dare to tread.

They come to the Land of Beulah.

And now they heard shouts rise up, for there was a noise in the town that a post came from The Celestial City with words of great joy for Christiana, the wife of Christian. So search was made for her, and the house was found in which she was.

Then the post put a note in her hands, the words of which were: "Hail, good Christiana! I bring you word that, the Lord calls for you, and waits for you to stand near His throne in robes of white, in ten days' time."

When he who brought the note had read it to her, he gave her a sign that they were words of truth and love, and said he had come to bid her make haste to be gone. The sign was a shaft with a sharp point, which was to tell her that at the time the note spoke of she must die.

Christiana heard with joy that her toils would so soon be at an end, and that she should once more live with her dear Christian.

She then sent for her sons and their wives to come to her. To these she gave words of good cheer. She told them how glad she was to have them near her at such a time. She sought to make her own death, now close at hand, of use to them, from this time up to the

hour when they should each of them have to leave this world. Her hope was that it might help to guide them on their path; that the faith which she had taught them to cling to, would have sunk deep in their hearts; and that all their works should spring from love to God. She could but pray that they would bear these words in mind, and put their whole trust in Him who had born their sins on the Cross, and had been slain to save them.

When the day came that she must go forth to the world of love and truth, the road was full of those who would yearn to see her start on her way; and the last words that she was heard to say were: "I come, Lord, to be with You."

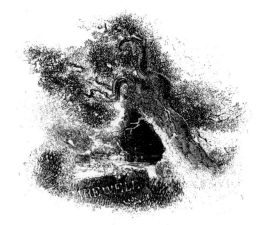